Dominion
Gods and Slaves Series

By

NICHOLAS BELLA

For information contact; address www.nicholasbella.com

Edited by Heidi Ryan of Amour The Line
Book Cover design by Jay Aheer of Simply Designs
Photographed models by Miky Merisi Photography

ISBN-13: 978-1546884347

ISBN-10: 1546884343

First Edition: August 2017

10 9 8 7 6 5 4 3 2 1

Books by Nicholas Bella:

Series

The New Haven Series

The Odin Chronicles

The Demon Gate Series

Cobra: The Gay Vigilante Series

The Gods and Slaves Series

The Circle of Darkness Series – W/Aimee Nicole Walker

Books (Collaborations)

Undisputed – W/Aimee Nichole Walker

Dedicated to my family, friends and fans who believed in me.

I love you all.

N.B.

PROLOGUE

O n the first day of January, in the year two-thousand and twelve, the world endured a catastrophe of epic proportions and lost over half its population. Billions perished during what became known as the Great Calamity, or The Gods' Revenge by the survivors. During the event, which took place at the same time all over the globe, the oceans swelled into waves over a hundred feet tall, creating the highest and most devastating tidal waves ever recorded in history. All lakes, ponds, and rivers rose, flooding lands and drowning people and animals.

The ground the world over shook and opened up, swallowing everything in the vicinity, even in locations that were not accustomed to earthquakes. Hurricanes, tornadoes, and typhoons ravaged the land and water. Volcanos erupted, spilling molting lava and ash on everyone as they fled for their lives. Fires burned what was left for days on end, destroying trees, homes, and killing more animals and humans.

Just when the survivors thought it was over, as they searched the smoldering rubble for their loved ones, their belongings, and some kind of semblance of a world they once knew—the second wave of the calamity hit. The ground began to shift, creating more natural disasters, killing even more of the population. The Earth began to reform itself as lands that had once been separated started to come back together. In thirty days, the world had less than a billion people left, all sharing one land under four gods.

Those four gods, the people quickly learned, were the God of Fire, Eloy, the God of Water, Odessa, the God of Wind, Simeon, and the God of Earth, Kijani. They had come to earth as they had done in the past over six millennia ago to cleanse the world of what they felt was its human corruption. That event of the past was known as the biblical great flood, where the story of Noah and his Ark became legend.

Although the gods had visited Earth during that time, they had not stayed. The Earth had been cleansed, new life could begin and their job had been completed. They succumbed to the flood they had created and their celestial forms returned to heaven. However, the message had been sent and the world began anew once the waters receded. For over six-thousand years, people flourished. They created new technologies that were just as wondrous as they were damaging.

For every advancement of the printing press, came the destruction of more trees. For every house that was made with granite counter tops, the Earth's core was weakened. For every resource that was syphoned from the planet, nature suffered. Animals went extinct or on endangered lists. People themselves were even considered resources for another man's will.

The gods watched it all unfold over those many millennia, seeing that even after their last intervention with the great flood, humanity had not learned its lesson. The four of them came to the conclusion that humans could not be trusted to hold domain over the kingdom that they'd been given. The fifth god—Hersi—the one who held dominion over all life—agreed. They knew that they had to do something, and that something came in the form of the Great Calamity.

However, they had to wait until the right moment to come back to Earth, as the level of havoc they wanted to wreak could only be done while they were on Earth and not in the heavens. Such was the rule set by the God Hersi. So, Odessa, Eloy, Simeon, and Kijani had to wait until human vessels were born into the world that could hold the sheer power of their celestial essence.

The moment came in the year two-thousand at the stroke of midnight. Only separated by a matter of hours and time zones, four humans came into this world stillborn, at first. Then to the doctors' surprise, life flowed into their tiny infant bodies. Unbeknownst to the parents and those doctors, four vengeful gods had just entered their realm. Once the gods reached the age of twelve, they finally had the strength to cleanse the world again, and they did. That day happened in two thousand-twelve.

This time, the gods didn't leave quietly as they had done before. This time, they didn't return to the God Hersi, thus disobeying Hersi's command, with severe consequences. Years after the Great Calamity, the gods' human bodies still continued to age, but at an extremely slow rate. It was the only failsafe Hersi had, not to make them immortal. Their celestial essence did preserve their human bodies well enough to have long lives, however.

During all this time, the four gods gave into the weaknesses of their human flesh. They indulged in their human emotions and desires. Where they had left the humans to their own devices before, now they wanted to be worshipped as the gods they were. The wanted the human devotion they felt they were owed. Their vanity took over and they exposed themselves to the humans who were still struggling to rebuild in a world that was devastated by every natural disaster known and unknown to man. Seeing true power before their very eyes gave the human race something else to believe in.

Eloy, Odessa, Kijani, and Simeon had united the survivors of the human race under one religion, but not everyone was willing to worship the four gods, and war broke out among the believers and the non-believers. A ten-year Godwar claimed even more lives, leaving less than half a billion people alive. Those who did not perish but still refused to worship the gods moved as far as they could from them into the desolate areas of each celestial city, which became known as the badlands.

The gods knew they had to keep control over the humans, so they established a new social order to create an elitist society. Those whom the gods deemed worthy, those humans who could give back to them the most, lived closer to their temples, which the humans built. And those the gods did not care about lived further away and had less resources and luxuries. This was a way to insure that humans would always want to worship and serve them and, above all, fear them. Because they were not immortal and could die, creating the new world this way meant they would remain protected.

With this new divine governing system in place, the humans did whatever they could to appease the gods and gain their favor. They learned that the gods shared in the same desires as they did, so the gods were honored with flesh for their sexual delights, artists to perform for their entertainment, and blood and sacrifice to sate their blood lust for sport.

The offering of the Games became the most desired by the gods. For them, it overshadowed all other forms of entertainment and encompassed them as well. For over two-hundred years, its popularity had only grown. Men and women would be captured, enslaved, and sold to ludi to be trained to fight in the main arena that connected all four cities. Some were born into the ludus and faced the same fate as any other slave of the ludus. With each victory, their respective ludus and city gained in favor from the gods. The battles were brutal, the crowd was viscous, and the gods were insatiable for it all.

And it is here where the tale of one man's trials and tribulations begin as he fights for his freedom from a world as cruel as it can be beautiful.

CHAPTER ONE

The waves of the sea were violently rocking the ship Mateo had been traveling in, so much so, he'd suffered horrible nausea for days now. He wasn't the only one with the ailment of sea sickness, as many other prisoners who'd been captured with him retched, gagged, and vomited their stomach contents on the floor and each other as they were packed so tightly together, no man had room to move.

Mateo's stomach lurched along with the waves, but he'd already purged himself of everything, which wasn't much to begin with since it had been his search for food that led his captors to him. Still, with the upheaval of the ship they were on, he only dry heaved as he prayed once more for death to take him. He didn't know where he was going, but he knew it wasn't anywhere he'd ever want to be. He'd listened to his captors talking amongst themselves about how much they'd make for their bounty. He knew he was going to be sold into slavery.

Whenever people went missing, it was almost always suspected to be the work of bandits. They would steal anything from exotic animals to grains to people. Anything that could be sold or traded. He feared that he'd never see his friends again, or his mother, Isabella, or his sister, Madeline. As the ship rocked from another ravaging wave, he thought back to the moment when his life changed.

He'd been out searching for food and other resources such as spices; these things were scarce in the badlands. Him being the only man in the house, it was his duty to provide. He'd gone looking for any animal he could find, armed with only a bow and several arrows he'd carved himself, he'd been determined to be successful. He'd traveled miles from his home towards the lushlands, and still hadn't found any rabbits, deer, or even a muskrat.

The land where he lived was so barren of resources, as they were as far away from the gods as one could get, it was a punishment to the people of the badlands that they should suffer the consequences of their blasphemy. To refuse to worship the gods, one would pay a hefty price. However, the perk of that price was that bandits didn't travel there much. The lack of resources, harsher weather conditions, and distance was often the deterrent.

It wasn't until they were forced to leave that safe zone in search of food that a badlander was at risk of being captured. That was what happened to him. Going into the lushlands where the grass was green, water fresh and clean, and animals were abundant put Mateo in the range of the bandits. He fought with everything he had, even killing one of the bandits that attacked him, but it was not enough. During the melee, he'd been struck with a rock from behind and rendered unconscious, only to wake up in the bowels of the ship with no knowledge of where he was going.

The other prisoners with him were all from surrounding badlands and were captured because they too had been searching for resources. For three days now, Mateo traveled on the sea to their new destinies and he feared what his future held. His body was cold on the inside even though it was hot in the ship, and he shivered as sweat dripped from his pores. His skin was dirty and smelled horrible, and the wound on the back of his skull throbbed. He wondered if it was infected and if so, perhaps he would be spared his fate and die from his wound. That was his hope, at least.

As they traveled, the waves began to work on him in a different way, lulling him to sleep, and he blissfully welcomed the unconscious reprieve. Finally, he was shaken awake by strong, brutal hands. When he opened his eyes, his vision cleared and he was looking into the face of one of his captors.

"We go," the man said as he began to undo the chains that kept him bound in place.

Mateo didn't know how long he'd been on the ship, as he was in and out of consciousness the entire time, but he did realize they were now docked. Another look around, he noticed the other captives being unchained… those who were still alive, that is. A great number of prisoners had died in transit. Some from festering wounds, others from sickness or starvation.

The man undoing Mateo's chains looked up at him, snarling as he scrunched up his nose. "Odessa's tits, you are foul in scent, like shit and piss and dirty cunt. But are pretty enough to fetch a nice price. Be happy that."

Mateo let the insult roll off him as he really didn't have the energy for a rebuttal. His stomach felt like an empty pit and he was still slightly nauseated from his journey. "Where... where are we?" he managed to ask through his painfully dry mouth and lips that were so cracked, they hurt.

"You are where you are," the man replied harshly. He snatched one of the chains that was connected to Mateo's iron collar, wrist and ankle cuffs. "Move!"

Mateo was yanked forward again, and ended up falling face first in the foul grime and muck on the floor. His body was far too weak to remain standing on its own, but he knew he had to try or possibly be dragged.

"Kijani's cock, pathetic. I'll not carry you. Move now!" the man barked his command.

Mateo struggled to push himself up onto his knees, which was proving to be one of the hardest things he'd ever done. Once he was able to sit on his knees, he gathered what little strength he had left and rose to his feet. With that, the man pulled on his chain, leading him out of the ship onto the deck. Mateo stumbled several times as he struggled to keep pace with the man, on legs that felt like wet noodles.

Mateo covered his eyes from the bright light of the sun's beaming rays. He'd been surrounded by darkness for so long, finally seeing light was almost a shock to his system. His captor yanked on his chain again, and he lurched forward, tripped, and fell onto the railing where he was able to catch his balance.

"Walk now!" the man ordered, not giving Mateo a chance to get his bearings.

Had Mateo had the strength, he would have attacked the man, the rage he felt at being captured and mistreated was all consuming, but he was far too weak to fight back. Instead, he put one foot in

Nicholas Bella

front of the other and allowed his captor to lead him to a large carriage where the other prisoners were being piled on. He climbed on and held on to one of the poles to keep from falling again.

He watched as his captor connected his chain to an iron hoop on the carriage, thus insuring he wouldn't be able to escape. The man walked back towards the ship to gather more slaves. Another male captive was led into the carriage and shackled to the iron hoop beside Mateo. The captive looked as broken down and exhausted as Mateo felt and looked. The bandit shoved the man to the floor and barked at him to "stay" as if he had choice. The man then walked off back to the ship.

Mateo counted how many bandits there were. Eight. How was it that eight men could enslave... he looked around the carriage and lost count after twenty-six men, women, and children? Not to mention, all the ones who'd died on the ship? Maybe there were more bandits that he hadn't got a chance to see, and only eight remained to continue to transport the prisoners.

Unable to stand any longer, he sank to the floor of the carriage, resting his head on the wood panel. The cool breeze on his skin was a welcomed aspect to his current situation as he'd been denied fresh air for days. As he sat there, his head resting on the carriage that would carry him to another uncertain fate, he felt forsaken and only wanted this nightmare to end. But he knew it was only beginning. Once all of the prisoners had been loaded into the carriage, to the point where there was no room for anyone to move or get completely comfortable, it began to move. It was more rocking and bumping, but nowhere near as tumultuous as the rocking of the ship, so Mateo counted what little blessings he did have.

"Where they get you from, you?" one of the prisoners asked him.

Mateo tore his gaze from the pretty white clouds in the blue sky to look at the man. "From the Kirrachi badlands."

The man smiled, revealing several rotten teeth. "Oh, me from Toredor badlands. Me was sleeping... they came into the badlands, they did... found me."

Mateo's eyes widened as his heart leaped into his throat at the knowledge that the bandits had entered the very badlands where they

8

hadn't before. "They came into the badlands?" he asked, his voice going up a pitch.

The man nodded. "They put bag over me head, they did. Me saw nothing... just heard. Heard screaming."

Mateo sighed woefully as he closed his eyes. The Toredor badlands were only a few dozen miles from the Kirrachi badlands where his family was. "Oh gods, please spare them," he prayed.

He knew for a fact that the gods did exist, as did everyone. For over two hundred years since the Great Calamity, the gods had made themselves known and had only granted certain people blessings. The people of the badlands were never so fortunate... but he could still hope.

"What they want with me and all us?" the man asked him.

Mateo looked at him. "I don't know."

"Too bad, for me want to know, me do," the man said, pouting.

"Me too," Mateo said, then he winced a little as he rubbed a sore spot on the back of his head.

"Me... me helped you, me did," the man said, pointing to Mateo's head.

Mateo continued to rub the sore spot, noting that the crusted blood was gone. He looked at his fingers, only seeing sweat and a few dried flakes of blood and what looked like old pus. He remembered then. He'd been so sick on the ship, passing in and out of consciousness and nauseated beyond all reason. His body had been feverish and he had hoped he would die without knowing he was dying. But of course, that hadn't happened as he was wide awake now and his sickness was fading.

"Yes... you almost goner, you. They let me save you, they did," the man said.

Mateo looked at him. "Why? Why you?"

The man shrugged. "Says you too pretty, they say." He grinned again. "Other say you killed bandit... you should suffer, they say." The man lifted his finger, digging it into his nose, and pulled a booger free from his nostril. Mateo resisted the urge to frown as the man ate the tiny, yellowish ball of dried snot. "Me good at fixing wounds, me am. You almost die, you did. Me told them me could save you, me did. They wanted to toss you over ship, they did."

The news that he had been spared a freeing death only to be saved for a worse fate didn't settle too well with Mateo as he thought about what it all meant. On the ship, he had been ready to die, but now… with new life flowing into him, he wasn't so sure. He still felt feverish, but not nearly as sick as he'd been before.

"Do you know how long we were at sea?" Mateo asked the man.

"Fifteen days, fourteen nights, me counted, me did," he replied.

Mateo looked at the man, his lip turned down in a frown. "I do not know if I should have gratitude for you saving my life or not."

"Ahhh, be nice, you. Me was happy to save you, me was" the man implored.

"Save me for what?" Mateo whispered softly to himself as he looked back up at the sky. Whatever was coming, he promised that he would live, if only to maybe one day see his family again.

CHAPTER TWO

The carriage stopped moving, which woke Mateo up. He hadn't even realized he'd drifted off to sleep again. He looked up, shocked by what he could see. The sun had long since set and the stars were shining brightly in the nighttime sky. Rising to his feet, he surveyed the area they were in. He could tell they were in the thick of a celestial city. Surrounding them were many buildings that were made of bricks, stone, and wood. Some were only a few stories tall, while others looked to be at least ten.

Ten stories was something to marvel at, which Mateo did as he peered up at them in awe. He'd heard stories of long ago cities, before the Great Calamity, with buildings so high, they reached into the clouds. He couldn't imagine seeing one that tall these days. How could one even build a structure that impressive? The area was heavily populated, which was something he wasn't used to, having lived in the badlands. People walked by their carriage and looked in as if they were examining the wares of a seller.

Mateo watched them as they looked over his body and those of the other prisoners. Other people who weren't interested in the new arrivals, continued to go about their business as they were free to do so. Seeing the difference in their statuses left Mateo with an even more foreboding feeling. They were in the marketplace to be sold off, no doubt.

Their bandit captors began unlocking their chains from the hoops on the carriage, one by one. As they were doing this, an older man with a graying beard and potbelly stepped up to the carriage. His eyes scanned over each one of the prisoners with a securitizing gaze. His clothes looked to be those of a man of some measure of wealth. Leather pants, boots, and a vest covering a white cotton, button down shirt. His salt and pepper hair was balding at the top and his gray eyebrows were bushy over his brown eyes.

He didn't look all too impressed with the prisoners in the carriage as he examined them, only a few managed to garner a grunt of approval, Mateo being one of them.

"Most are so thin," he said. "The children especially."

The lead bandit stepped up to him. "We went into the badlands for this lot, sir. Many fled...some we caught in the lushlands."

The lushlands were where they'd captured Mateo as he was hunting. The lushlands were full of resources and plenty of people lived there, but as they were far from the temple of the gods, they didn't have as much protection from the gods. Bandits hunted the lushlands regularly, so it was a risk to live there and hunt there. If you didn't want to be captured, you lived in the badlands because prior to this incident, bandits didn't go past the lushlands to get to the badlands.

All that was changing now as it would seem people were becoming a more sought after commodity than before. Mateo listened to the two men talk about them as if they were mere objects void of emotions. It was another cruel reminder of the reality that had befallen him.

"Bring them, the auction starts in a few minutes," the older man said, then he walked away, leaving the head bandit to his charge.

"You all come now, no fighting or you die," he warned.

Mateo wanted to fight, but the threat of certain death kept him from trying. Also, he was bound in chains and connected to several prisoners with no real means of escape. So, like the others, he climbed down from the carriage and followed the prisoners as they shuffled towards a large, wooden platform where many people were gathered.

The adult prisoners were told to stand on the side while six children were led onto the stage. Their tiny bodies were covered in dirt and muck, much like the other prisoners, except for the clean streaks on their cheeks left by their tears. One of the children's mother tried to reach out to her son as he was led up to the platform, but she was punched in her stomach by one of the bandits, causing her to double over from the pain of the blow.

"Stupid whore! He not yours no more," the man growled as he shoved the crying child forward and pushed her back against the wall.

Mateo remembered seeing them both on the ship, they had been separated then, too. And even on the carriage ride over, the bandits had chained the children apart from the adults. He guessed that was their way of making sure she and her child understood they'd better get used to being separated.

Mateo watched his first ever auction take place. He'd heard of such things growing up, but until this moment, had been able to avoid it. Living far away from the gods' temples had its disadvantages and advantages. The older man with the rich clothes who'd inspected them earlier stood on the platform to address the crowd.

"We have a fine lot for you tonight, a fine lot," he boasted, which was odd to Mateo since he'd clearly heard the man complaining about them while still in the carriage. The man continued. "We start off first with these children. They are young and can be trained to do your bidding without much fight."

"I could use some in my brothel," one of the patrons said.

Mateo looked at the woman and shivered in disgust when he saw how lecherous her gaze was as she looked at the young boys and girls. He knew that slaves had no rights, and the whims and desires of those considered elite or blessed had no conscience. These were all lessons his mother had taught him, and she'd learned those lessons from her mother, and so on. Knowledge handed down through the generations to keep them safe.

The man on stage continued to promote the children he wanted to sell. He walked over to one of the children, grabbing him by the chain on his neck. The chain connected all of the children together, so not one could get away. He yanked the child forward and the boy stumbled as he moved into position. His blue eyes were cast downward, avoiding the crowd as his little body trembled in fear.

"Look this one, so young...so fair. He's pretty, make a nice servant in any house," the man said, then he reached down, grabbing the boy's chin, and forced him to look up at the crowd so they could see his face.

There were some murmurs from those gathered as they looked over the children. Mateo was afraid for his own fate, but even he couldn't fathom what those children were going to go through. Being young, would they be easily broken? Would they survive whatever their owners had in store? He didn't want to think about it and turned away once the bidding started.

The customers and seller haggled over the price, many wanted bargains and didn't think the children were worth the asking price. There was much debate, but in the end, everyone—except the children—were satisfied with their purchase and sale. Once the children were led away, the women were dragged onto the stage.

Again, the seller went into bragging about his human wares. They were all naked, so it was easy for the customers to see exactly what they were buying. The seller lifted up the breasts of the heavier-chested women and patted the breasts of the daintier-chested women, showing the crowd their worth. The women were made to turn around and bend over, exposing their private parts.

The crowd made remarks, many nodding in approval right before the bidding started again. One by one, and in some cases, two by two, the women were sold off to their new owners. Some were going to serve the moderately wealthy, while others were going to serve in brothels, baths, and public labor, such as maintaining public toilets or streets.

Now, it was the men's turn to be auctioned off. Like the children and women before them, the chains around their necks had been connected the moment they had stepped off the carriage, and not one of them could free themselves from the others. Mateo followed in line onto the stage and stood before the crowd of over sixty people, all looking at them with ill intent.

No decent human being could own another, was what his mother had told him. Everyone should want freedom and grant it to others. She didn't believe in the way things were, which was the reason why she wanted to raise her children in the badlands away from the bustle of the worshippers of the gods, which she had refused to believe in because of their cruelty and exploitation of others.

Mateo looked around, seeing the city that was thriving under the control of the gods; and everywhere he looked, he saw corruption, greed, lust, and vanity. He'd heard the ancient tales of why the gods had destroyed the old world, but what he was seeing now didn't seem any different. The only exception was that the gods were now in control. What kind of gods were these?

"Look at these strong men… they serve you well," the seller said. Then he instructed the prisoners to turn around and bend over.

Mateo felt degradation for the first time in his life when he had to expose his genitalia for all to see. He could hear the people talking amongst themselves, judging them, and he wanted to cry. It took every ounce of pride in him to not let one single tear fall. He didn't want to give them the satisfaction. He didn't want them to break him, and his chest tightened with his resolve.

After bending over, they were instructed to turn back around and face the crowd as the bidding began. Most of the males went relatively quickly for cheap. Only a handful stood out from the rest according to the seller, Mateo being one of them. Two brothel owners were bidding for him. The seller went back and forth, raising the price until another party joined, raising the price even more.

Mateo looked at the man who happened to be wearing fine clothing like the seller. He looked to be with a bodyguard as there was a tall, muscular, black man standing at his side, looking quite menacing in a tan toga. With the man's final bid, the other two opted out and Mateo was sold just like that. Two more men were purchased along with him, and they looked even more broken down than Mateo. Their skin was marred with fresh wounds, some were scabbing over, and Mateo could tell they'd been beaten. With that final purchase, that was the end of the auction.

The chains were linked around Mateo's neck and the two men he was sold with, and they were led off the stage to their new owner. Now that Mateo was standing before the man, he got a good look at him. He looked to be in his mid-forties with a bit of a pudge around the waist. Black hair, graying at the sides, a beard and mustache and sharply arched eyebrows that hooded over deep blue eyes. His jawline was chiseled and set as he looked over the men he'd just purchased.

"This stock not so bad, dominus," the guard said to his master.

The man's lips turned up in a sneer. "Eh, I've had better. This lot will do. Cervantes has his work cut out for him, if they pass the test," the man said as his eyes roamed over his new purchases. "Bring them." With that command, he turned and walked towards a beautiful black steed, climbing onto the animal's back.

The black guard led the slaves behind their new master by their connected chain. Mateo's feet ached as he walked over sharp pebbles and hard gravel while they traveled for miles towards their new home. He knew his feet were bleeding, could see his bloody footprints as they trekked. Of course, the other men's feet were bleeding as well, but no one said anything, knowing their words would fall on deaf ears.

He looked up at his new owner, the man was riding comfortably on his black horse, looking as lofty as so many of the people here did. These were the people his mother had told him stories about. Those clamoring for the favor of the gods. Many had sacrificed much to gain such attention for the four celestial beings who now controlled the entire world. The gods didn't pay these people any attention, his mother had told him. All the gods wanted was to be worshipped, and as long as the people worshipped them, they allowed the people to live.

These people looked down on the people of the badlands as heretics deserving of whatever fate they were given. Mateo knew he'd find no mercy. He'd find no compassion at the hands of his new owner and he only hoped that his mother and sister were safe.

The man before him collapsed, which dragged him and the other man to the ground. As expected, their new owner had no sympathy for the three men who'd been kidnapped from their land, starved, beaten in some cases, and now sold. He didn't care for their weary, aching muscles, sore feet and overall exhaustion.

"Get them up!" he barked.

"Yes, dominus," the black servant replied, then he reached for the whip attached to his belt and the sound of the whip cracking shook Mateo to his core before he felt its biting sting. He cried out, back arching in pain. "Rise, now!" the servant yelled, right before he whipped the other two men in quick succession, giving each one blow. The men cried out in pain just as Mateo had done, and it was enough for them to struggle to their bleeding feet once more.

Once all were standing, they continued on their journey. Mateo had long since lost track of the time. He only knew that the trip seemed endless and he actually thanked a god when they finally arrived. It was one of the biggest dwellings he'd ever seen. Huge compared to the thin wood hut he and his family had lived in.

The badlands wasn't a place where people had roomy homes. Wood or straw huts or tents were the norm. Seeing the two-story brick structure was a definite step up. He looked up at the balcony where two people, who were obviously servants based on their lack of clothing, looked down on them. They looked to be wearing only short tunics pinned at their shoulders and leather belts at their waists. He couldn't see their feet, but he figured they might be wearing sandals.

"Get them ready for introductions," their owner commanded.

"Yes, dominus," the servant obediently replied, then his gaze shifted to the new prisoners. "Stand straight, present yourself to your new dominus!"

Mateo didn't know what he meant by presenting himself, but he managed to straighten his spine, which was aching from all he had already endured. The other two men stood as straight as they could, considering how exhausted and hurt they were. The new wound from the whip on Mateo's back burned as the wind, sweat, and more dirt got into it. As much as he didn't want to admit it, a part of him was thinking that he was cursed as punishment for living in the badlands. For refusing to worship the gods.

The man who purchased them stood quietly as his servant gave orders to other servants. Mateo watched their actions, as well as took in his new surroundings. They were in a courtyard surrounded by four very tall brick walls, but no roof. There was one entrance and exit, which they had entered through. That gate was now locked and guarded by a man with a metal chest plate, leather pants, and a sword at his hip. The other wall featured two cells with barred doors. The third wall had three windows that were also barred, and the forth wall had two doors, one that led into the main house and the other that led to a one-story addition to the main house that was connected by a short hallway.

Escape would be difficult, if not impossible. Mateo continued his inspection, there was a crest engraved in the wall over the balcony with the letter "R" in the intricate design. Mateo couldn't tell how big the main house truly was from the courtyard, not without going inside, but two stories said a lot. He looked at the adjacent section of the house and wondered what that led to.

All of a sudden, the door to the one-story dwelling opened and more men began to enter the courtyard. The men were led by a hulking man dressed in modest clothing of leather pants, a linen pullover shirt, and sandals. The man looked to be in his sixties and at least six-four. His head was bald, but he had a gray beard and mustache. His steel gray eyes peered at the new men his master had just acquired, but his expression remained unreadable. He lined the other men up to be presented to their dominus as instructed.

Mateo looked at them as they all filled the area, standing opposite him in a straight line. These men looked well fed, their robust bodies were rippling with muscles that were very impressive. Their skin had a healthy glow under the oil that was now glistening on their flesh in the moonlight. By the position that one guy took, the one who had led the men into the courtyard, Mateo could tell he held rank among them.

Another thing that was interesting to Mateo was how the men were dressed. Some of them wore loincloths of different colors and styles, such as leather straps hanging down or satin. Others were wearing tunics or leather shorts. All had sandals to protect their feet, some with short straps and others with longer ones that crisscrossed up their legs. Mateo wondered why they didn't all dress the same.

Their new owner stepped up then, waving his hand at the muscular men standing silently behind him. Their gazes bored into Mateo and the other two men as if they were unworthy to be in the same room. Mateo stared back, refusing to let them make him feel shame. He never asked to be there in the first place… whatever this place was.

The men's gazes were extremely intimidating, but Mateo kept his stance even though he did feel fear as they looked at him. It made him wonder just what kind of slaves they were to be so menacing. The men's bodies all carried scars and some had tattoos. All were taller than Mateo was; as a matter of fact, Mateo was the shortest of all the men present, including the slaves he was chained to. That alone was impressive, because Mateo stood six-feet tall, which meant these other men were goliaths.

That begged the question again… where was he?

CHAPTER THREE

"These men are what you need to strive to be," their owner said in his deep baritone. "They are the pride of my house... the House of Rama!"

"All hail Rama!" the men shouted in unison in a boisterous chorus and they thrust their fists in the air.

The roar coming from them surprised Mateo, since he wasn't expecting it. Some of the men laughed at him when they saw him and the other men jump in response to their devotion to their master. If nothing else could be gathered from this moment, at least Mateo now knew the name of the man who'd purchased him like he was a pair of shoes: Rama.

Rama walked over to them, standing before Mateo. "You are soft on the eyes and the only reason I purchased you, that and your youth. The gods will like that. Your body..." he reached out, poking Mateo's biceps and abs, "needs buffering and bulking. Not too much, I don't think. Your size is nice." He wrinkled up his nose and frowned. "You all need bathing, but not till you prove yourselves worthy of the god's water."

"P—please...we t—thirsty," one of the other prisoner's begged.

Rama's head turned sharply towards the man who had so rudely addressed him. He walked over to the man, who was swaying a little as he strained to keep standing.

"Are you thirsty, slave?" Rama asked.

The man nodded. "Y—yes," he replied through dry, chapped lips.

"Kneel," Rama commanded.

The man dropped to his knees in front of Rama. Mateo and the other prisoner watched in silence as the black servant came to stand behind the kneeling man as their owner began to undo his pants.

"No! No p—please," the slave protested.

"Silence, filth!" Rama yelled, quieting the man. "You are not worthy of the blessings of the gods. So, you will only get what man can give you until you prove yourselves tomorrow, if you survive." He pulled his stubby, uncut cock out from his pants and aimed it at the man's face. "Open your mouth."

Mateo turned away, not wanting to see what was going to happen next. He looked at the other men who were standing and observing what was going on. Not one tried to help and some were even laughing and smirking.

"Watch!" Rama's baritone snapped Mateo's attention back to him. "You're next."

Mateo was as thirsty as a man could be, but he didn't want what Rama was offering. "Dominus, I am not thirsty," he lied, but he hoped that with the level of respect he gave the man, that he might... might spare him.

"I did not ask if you were thirsty," Rama said. "If I choose to piss down your throat, you will drink it greedily and say 'gratitude, dominus', comprehend?"

Mateo wanted to vomit at the thought, but his stomach had been empty for days. This was his life now, would he accept it? Could he? He was only nineteen, and never had he ever thought he'd be in this predicament. He'd heard how horrible the life of a slave could be, that they had no rights. That they were just property of their masters. It was a life he never wanted for himself, but he knew he had to obey if he didn't want to be punished. Adjustment was necessary for survival.

Not wanting to anger his master, he nodded. "Yes, dominus."

Rama turned his attention back to the man kneeling before him. The black servant was now holding the man's mouth open and Rama released his yellow stream. The servant struggled to spit it out, and that seemed to anger Rama even more.

"Drink it, filth! Or next, I shit down your throat!" Rama shouted.

That threat seemed like it was enough motivation for the man as he began to swallow the urine his master gave him. "Good... yes... drink it all... so you're not thirsty anymore."

When Rama's stream began to trickle, he placed the tip of his cock inside the man's mouth. "Now... clean."

Mateo could tell by how their dominus moaned that he was enjoying the feeling of the man's mouth on his cock. After he was satisfied, he pulled his cock from the man's mouth and stuffed it back into his pants, zipping them up.

Rama looked at the black man who'd been holding the other man's mouth open. "Kodac…" He turned to the man standing by the line of muscular men. "Cervantes, relieve these men of their thirst," he said, gesturing to Mateo and the other prisoner.

Mateo watched as the man who'd led the other slaves out there walked toward him. He didn't know if he could drink this man's piss, but he knew he wouldn't want the latter, no matter how hungry he was. The black servant who had brought them there came around the front to the other man and began undoing his linen pants.

The other prisoner looked at Mateo, eyes wide and mouth turned down in a disgusted frown, but he didn't try to protest. They'd already been warned of what would happen if they refused to drink. Mateo's own expression mirrored the other man's, and he swallowed hard, which took some effort as his mouth was dry, but he did so to fight the nausea that rolled through his stomach.

"Kneel, filth," Rama ordered.

Mateo and the other prisoner obeyed and dropped down to their knees in front of the two men standing before them.

"Look up at us," Cervantes commanded.

Both men's gaze shot up to stare into the cruel eyes of the men who were about to piss down their throats. Kodac's cock was long, uncut, thick, and dark with a pinkish tip and deep slit. Cervantes was shorter, uncut, and thinner, but just as threatening to Mateo as Kodac's bigger one. He counted his little blessing that it was Cervantes whose cock he'd have to drink from.

"Open your mouths," Cervantes ordered.

They did, even though neither man wanted to. Mateo's body was tense as he anticipated the rancid taste of the other man's urine. The moment the hot liquid hit his tongue, he jerked back, the stream splashing him in the face. He closed his eyes and turned his face to wipe the urine away.

"Get back here!" Cervantes roared. Fear seized Mateo and he returned to his position, mouth open to take the rest. "Swallow it!"

It took all of his strength to drink the piss. In spite of the grossness of their situation, neither man couldn't deny that the liquid did sate their painful thirst. Mateo tried to think of it as just one more thing he'd have to do to survive as he guzzled down the hot, bitter stream. Some of it dripped down his chin, but that didn't seem to bother Cervantes.

"Yeah, I was holding that in my balls for a while now… saving it just for you," Cervantes taunted as he purposely jerked his dick up to aim his stream in Mateo's face. Mateo closed his eyes again to keep the piss from getting in them as Cervantes laughed. "Look at me when you drink my piss, boy." Mateo forced his eyes open and looked up at the wicked man who was obviously delighting in the debasing as he aimed his piss-flowing cock at Mateo's mouth.

Out of the corner of his eye, Mateo could see the other prisoner drinking Kodac's piss, which seemed to burst from his slit like a geyser. The prisoner choked on the flow twice, but manage to drink enough to not enrage their new owner, who stood and watched the entire thing. The other slaves laughed or whispered among themselves as they watched. A few only looked on with unreadable expressions, while a handful had disgust on their faces. Perhaps remembering when they'd had to go through it. At least, that was what Mateo suspected.

Finally, Cervantes flow slowed to a trickle and he did as their owner had done. He placed the tip of his cock inside Mateo's mouth, and having seen what was expected already, Mateo sucked and licked the man's slit clean of piss while the man moaned in delight.

"Yeeess, that is nice. Lick it clean, filth," Cervantes said, then he began to push his cock deeper into Mateo's mouth, taking Mateo by surprise as he gagged when the tip of the man's cock hit the back of his throat.

"Cervantes," Rama said.

The man immediately removed his cock from Mateo's mouth and took a step backward. "My apologies, dominus."

"Do not get overzealous with this lot. Not until they prove themselves worthy of the gods and my coin. These men cost me three-hundred rubios… they will earn it one way or another," Rama said.

Mateo knew how much three-hundred rubios was. Sadly, it wasn't much. Several kids had gone for four hundred rubios alone. Rama had spent less than that on three men. If Mateo didn't already feel low, that knowledge only made him despair more. So little was he valued. So little were they all valued. Maybe if he or his family had had that much money, he could have bought his freedom.

"You did adequate taking my stream, filth," Kodac said as he pulled his massive meat from the other prisoner's mouth.

"You piss like a horse, Kodac," Rama announced with a boisterous laugh. "This slave surely has a belly full—yes."

"He does, dominus," Kodac agreed.

Mateo looked at the man from out of the corner of his eye again, noting the sweaty, pale complexion turning a bit green. The man looked like he would spew up the urine at any moment. A terrible thing if he did, Mateo concluded. His own stomach rolled at the thought of what was now sloshing inside of it. Still, he fought to keep his nausea at bay.

Both Kodac and Cervantes stood to the side once again while Rama took to the center to address the new prisoners. "You have a new destiny before you. One that can offer you greatness if you desire it hard enough, or death if you do not. I am your dominus and this is my ludus. The men you see here before you are all my gladiators. Warriors of the arena and they spill blood to honor the gods and this ludus."

"All hail dominus!" the men shouted in unison once again, and that seemed to please Rama, as his chest poked out a bit more.

He looked at Mateo and the other two men. "Tomorrow afternoon is the monthly games. As new prospects, you will present yourselves to the gods and face off with a warrior from my stable. If you survive, you will have proven yourself worthy of the gods and my stable. If you survive the first test, you will train to become a gladiator under Cervantes, your doctore." He pointed to the man who Mateo knew more intimately than he wanted.

"The honor is mine, dominus," Cervantes said, then his cold, hard gaze settled on Mateo and the other two men. "If these filthies prove themselves competent and worthy of the gods, that is."

Rama nodded. "Yes, if." He continued to address the prisoners. "You will face off with Haraka."

When he mentioned the name of their opponent, the gladiators standing behind him burst into joyous shouts and several men patted one of them on the back. Mateo figured the one getting the congratulatory praise was Haraka. The man he was supposed to fight and possibly kill in less than twenty-four hours, or at least die trying.

"See how happy my gladiators are to serve me and the gods?" Rama asked them.

"Yes, dominus," Mateo said.

"Y-yes, dominus," the other two men echoed, once they realized their blunder.

"Answer your dominus faster next time. Such a delayed response could prove terrible for filth like you," Cervantes barked.

"Apologies, dominus!" the two men said immediately after the reprimand.

"As I said, if you survive, you train, and if you survive training, you become gladiators of the celestial city of Fiary," Rama said.

Fiary, so that was where they were. Mateo had been trying to gather that information since being kidnapped. Fiary was the city of the celestial God of Fire, Eloy. He didn't know much about the gods, not really, having been born and raised far away from the celestial lands, which was where all of their temples resided in their respective cities. The celestial lands was also where the richest of the rich lived as well. Mateo came from the badlands of Airies, and the god of that city was Simeon. No wonder they had traveled for so many days. Mateo was a far distance from his home.

Their new owner looked at them, his frown deepening to show his disgust. "I do not have high hopes for you tomorrow. I think you all will meet your deaths. Whatever training you have, put it to use, as Haraka is well-taught. If you survive, you sleep inside the gladiator's wing. But until then, you rest… outside." He pointed to one of the cells built into the wall that looked to be very cramped and didn't have any amenities. It would have been cruel to put a rodent in there, let alone three humans.

Cervantes and Kodac approached the three men, taking their chains, forcing them to rise. They walked them towards the cell with its rusty, metal bars. The prisoners were shoved in and the door was locked behind them. The space was restrictive, leaving them only enough room to lay in fetal positions on the sandy ground. Mateo sat down on the floor, his back to the wall, knees drawn up. He kept his gaze on the activity going on the other side of his bars.

Cervantes leaned close to the bars, grinning down at the men. He was missing several teeth and one was rotten, which didn't help the scent of his breath. His gray gaze settled on Mateo and his smile turned more lecherous. "I hope you survive, pretty one. I want you to taste my cock until I shoot my ball milk down your gullet." He grabbed his crotch for added emphasis.

Mateo looked up at the man, he didn't bother to comment or even snarl, which was what he wanted to do. He knew he didn't have any power here and he was far too weak, tired, and hungry to put up any fight. The doctore laughed, then hacked up a glob of phlegm and spat it at Mateo. The mess landed on his right shoulder. Mateo jerked and looked at the revolting spit that was now sliding down his skin. He turned his disgusted gaze toward Cervantes as the man continued to laugh.

"Lick that if you're still thirsty," Cervantes said, then walked away, scratching his balls.

Mateo wiped the spit from his shoulder with the back of his hand and rubbed the mess into the sandy ground. He'd never felt such revulsion as he had in the little time he'd been in company of his new owner. Savages, all of them as far as Mateo was concerned. They were all alone now, everyone had gone back inside the building and it was just the three of them, locked in the hellish little cell.

"Do you think we will survive the battle tomorrow?" one of the prisoners asked. His voice was shaky with the terror he felt.

"We are forsaken," the other replied. "We face off with a seasoned warrior. One who has had food in his belly and rest. None of which we have had. We are doomed." The man rested his head against the cold metal bars and closed his eyes, as if he'd already given up.

The other man looked at Mateo. "Do you think we die tomorrow?"

His future was something he didn't really want to think about. It was so unpredictable and he wasn't even sure if he wanted a future as a gladiator if he were to survive. Of course, surviving was the name of the game, and if he was to think about his future, maybe it might be worth fighting for. He was conflicted.

Mateo looked at the frail man, the one who'd had begged for water and gotten them all punished. "There is only hope," he said, though if he'd been honest, Mateo didn't think the man had a chance of survival. But hope was all any of them had at this point. The three of them ceased their conversation and tried their best to get some rest.

CHAPTER FOUR

E loy lounged in the massive tub, enjoying the touch of the human servants who tended to him. One pretty male washed his back while another bathed his chest. Both servants remained silent, as they knew that humans were only to speak in a god's presence when spoken to.

Eloy's piercing amber gaze traveled over the lithe body of the male servant in front of him who was running the sponge down the length of his chest towards his cock. The human chanced a glance at Eloy's face and quickly averted his gaze, his cheeks blushing from having locked eyes with such a powerful, beautiful, and majestic being.

"Do you enjoy bathing me?" Eloy asked. Of course, he already knew the answer. The highlight of this human's day, and the other still washing his back, was being in his presence, let alone touching his flesh.

The human smiled. "Yes, my Celestial God."

Eloy smirked, pleased with the response he had been expecting. He moaned as the humans began to bathe his ass and groin. His cock was fat and long, with thick veins cording their way through his impressive member. The head of his cock was quite bulbous with a deep slit and whenever he shot off a load, it was always plentiful, enough to fill a cup. Of course, his seed was never to be wasted and there was always a hungry mouth or asshole to shoot his seed into.

Even now, as he was being cleansed, the human flesh that encased his celestial essence began to respond of its own volition to the gentle strokes and caresses he was receiving from the servants. Even after two-hundred plus years, he was still at the mercy of his body's desire for food, comfort, excitement, and above all, pleasure.

The human servant looked up at Eloy, just shy of making full eye contact. His expression relayed his question, and Eloy nodded. The human smiled and began to stroke the hard cock in his hand. Eloy closed his eyes and allowed himself to enjoy the fingers now eagerly coaxing an orgasm from him. The human was doing a decent job, although Eloy had had better just an hour earlier from another slave from his harem.

The other male continued to bathe his legs, having to go under the water to do so. He came up every so often for fresh air. He did that until he was done, then he stepped back and stood quietly while the other servant continued to jerk Eloy off.

"Ahhhhhh." Eloy released the long sigh as his balls tightened. The slave's fingers rubbed his cock head nicely, which brought him closer to climax. The servant dipped under the water, taking Eloy's cock into his mouth as he continued to stroke the god. Eloy let his head fall back and he groaned deeply as his body released into the male's mouth. "Mrrrmm." Eloy's body jerked several times as he groaned and grunted until the last of his seed had left his cock.

The male servant stood up, his body dripping with the soapy water. He swallowed Eloy's cum, then stepped back and bowed his head. "Thank you for your celestial seed, God Eloy," the servant said.

Eloy smiled as he reached up, caressing the male's tender cheek. "A mouth and throat should be so blessed."

"Yes, God Eloy," the servant agreed and swallowed again, tasting the last of Eloy's semen.

Pleased with the attention he'd received, Eloy dismissed them with the wave of his hand. "Leave me."

"Yes, Celestial God," the two said, then they left Eloy alone.

Using the marble stairs, he climbed out of the large, round, red tub that took up most of the space in his luxurious bathroom made of white marble with red veining. His toilet was red, as were his double sinks. He had a shower as well, which contained six nozzles that rained down the water, which he thoroughly enjoyed.

Snatching a towel off the rack, he began to dry himself. Normally, he'd leave such a task to his human servants, but he'd had enough of them for the night, having spent most of the day fucking. All he wanted to do now was climb into his huge comfortable bed and sleep for many hours. He'd been particularly horny and had needed the release multiple times, as was the case when the Games were near. Eloy loved the gladiatorial matches of the Games, even more than Kijani did.

Of course, Simeon didn't favor them, but attended to show solidarity. Odessa loved them as much as he did, and oftentimes, would fuck the winners of each match that night. Hell, they both did in what they later called the Championship Orgy. It was one thing the gladiators who participated in the games looked forward to. Everyone knew that having sex with a god was a lifechanging experience, and one wanted to be so sanctified.

"Fortune favored the gods and was favored by the gods," Eloy whispered to himself as he stared at his brilliance in the large ceiling to floor mirror. It was the motto that all gladiators trained under. The belief that if they won their matches, they were worthy of the gods' favor. A gladiator's success didn't just end with him, but his master and the city that they also represented.

Many felt it was honorable to die in the arena, as their deaths meant something to the gods who witnessed their sacrifice. And it did. To die in service of pleasing the gods was victory in and of itself, and even those ludi whose gladiators fell in the arena received the gods' blessings. Of course, that was only if the gladiator gave a glorious showing in the arena. A poor showing could prove to be disastrous for not only that ludus, but for the people of that particular celestial city.

Each of the four gods possessed certain abilities that pertained to the elements and if they were displeased with the worship or offerings of the people, then they could refuse to bless the people with their favor. So, there would be no wind to cool people in the blistering heat. Or in other areas, there may be too much wind, which would destroy many buildings, or worse. Many would suffer and die if Simeon was so inclined to withhold his blessings. Or, maybe it was Eloy himself that was unimpressed with the offering. That meant people would lack the ability to create fire, as he controlled it all. Many might freeze to death or starve in some cases.

Pleasing the gods and keeping in their good graces was of the utmost importance to their worshippers. Which was why the Games became the focal point of such a presentation of offerings. The blood, the rush of the battle, and the excitement of the crowd seemed to fuel the gods' desires, and every month, new offerings were presented in the arena.

Eloy was anxious about the upcoming Games. He wanted to see which ludus would come out victorious, as each of the four cities had to present their own gladiators for the Games. In each city, it contained more than one ludus, each competing for the ultimate position of the best in the city. To gain extra favor, a ludus might present new slaves to endure the Trial of Fate. These untrained men or women would face a trained gladiator or more in a fight to the death. Either victorious or not, their fates had been chosen. It was something that Eloy had taken quite an interest in. The last Games had no such presentation and had disappointed him, which prompted the humans to find new slaves.

In the past, Eloy had been impressed with Rama's gladiators. In his opinion, they were some of the best trained he'd seen. Perhaps equal to the strapping gladiators of Olafey's ludus from Odessa's city, Ocena. Nevertheless, he was excited to see what would happen at the Games. Would anyone stand out as a possible champion, one worthy of participating in the orgy? Only time would tell.

Eloy tossed the towel to the floor, then walked into his lavish master bedroom. The large four poster bed that sat in the middle of the room on a raised dais had seen its fair share of sweaty, male flesh and Eloy was determined to add more between the sheets. If there was one thing he loved about being inside a human's encasement, it was the pleasure that body yielded.

Even something as simple as a caress or kiss could send him spiraling into a vortex of ecstasy. He could see why humans had succumbed to their whims so easily. Not that he could forgive them for taking advantage of the paradise they'd been given. But he could understand why one had so many desires.

As for the paradise, well, that belonged to them now. Him, Kijani, Simeon, and Odessa. The humans needed more guidance only they could provide. If anyone was to rule the masses, the four gods decided it should be them. Everything was much better now, as far as they were concerned.

Well, that wasn't entirely true. Simeon, who'd been on board with their plan in the beginning, had grown to see things differently over the decades. Oftentimes, he'd chastised the other gods for their cruelty and tried to reason with them to show more mercy to their worshippers, but because he stood alone, he was always outvoted, so to speak.

Still, and for their own survival, he stood with them as a show of unity and, after the ten year Godwar, they were never challenged. As they knew they wouldn't be. Humans feared real power and they instinctually bowed down to it. Gone were the days of the past where they prayed to unseen forces.

Now, they knew who they prayed to and why. Faith was replaced with reality and fear. The humans hoped that the gods would continue to bless them. Only a few humans, too few for the gods to concern themselves with, refused to conform. They lived far away from what was considered civilized society and the blessed lands of the cities.

Certain areas within each city contained these "badlands". Desolate areas the gods did not consider sacred, but in spite of that, seemed to thrive in other ways. Sure, the people had to venture far for resources and somehow managed to survive off of self-made ones, but those lands were hellish as they lacked a sufficient water source and didn't receive very much rain.

The earth under their feet wasn't rich enough to grow fruits or vegetables. The air was dry and could be very hot in the day and cold at night. Fire was something that was also hard to come by, as Eloy didn't always allow it, but to appease Simeon, the other three gods would grant little mercies, if you will, to the people in the badlands. Perhaps that was why they were able to survive over the many decades since the gods had taken control.

In any case, Eloy was intrigued by the people of the badlands. His interest remained that of one who watches as ants go about their day carrying out their duties, nothing more. Every so often, like that casual observer watching the ants going to and from their ant hill, he had the urge to crush it under foot. The wicked glee he'd get from that would be entertaining, but promises were made to Simeon, so he and the others were forced to let the people of the badlands be.

However, those people were not protected under their edict. So, whatever the humans did to their own didn't concern them. Not every human wanted to sacrifice themselves in the arena or be trained in the many bordellos that littered the four cities, each boasting their own particular fleshy delights to appease the gods. With that in mind, the gods knew that slavery was a necessity, and one that gave them what they wanted. So no, they did not interfere.

Eloy crawled into his bed with its extremely comfortable, handwoven sheets and blanket. He settled in and closed his eyes, then drifted off to sleep with the thoughts of tomorrow's Games at the front of his mind. He hoped the humans could produce something he hadn't seen, or at least something that would be exciting.

CHAPTER FIVE

The sound of keys clanking against metal woke Mateo and the other two prisoners up. He opened his eyes, rubbing them a little as he focused his vision on the man opening their cell. It was Cervantes, the doctore, and if he survived the day's events, maybe his new trainer.

"Get up and move asses," Cervantes commanded.

Mateo and the others rose to their feet, weakly as they had been starved of food for days. In all honesty, Mateo wasn't sure how he would be able to fight a trained gladiator who was not weakened or dehydrated like he was, and still hope to survive at the end. He would surely need the favor of the gods, and he didn't see that happening.

A part of him wanted to be resolved to his fate that death awaited him in a few short hours. But the other half of him wanted to fight with everything he had. Only time would tell when he entered that arena, which half of him would take the reins. His stomach grumbled as he exited the cell, and he pressed his hand on his abdomen as if to quiet it.

Once all three were out of the cell, Cervantes connected another chain to the loop on their collars, and then attached that to the metal loop on a carriage. Inside the carriage were seven gladiators, Haraka being one of them. Each man seemed to be carrying his own fighting gear in netted sacks, but no weapons. The men looked at them from the semi-comfort of the carriage and laughed.

"Keep up your pace or be dragged. We're not gonna stop for you, comprehend?" Cervantes warned.

"Yes, doctore," Mateo said, understanding what was said. He didn't know if he had the strength to keep up with the carriage he was now attached to, but he'd try.

Cervantes' gaze traveled to the other two men who repeated what Mateo had said with nods of their heads. His lips drew up in a sneer. "Your voices gone?"

"Apologies, doctore," the two men said.

"Good, answer me."

"Yes, doctore," they said.

Satisfied, Cervantes turned and began addressing the gladiators sitting inside the carriage. There was another carriage waiting as well, this one far grander looking than the one the gladiators were riding in, which looked more standard. A simple bench with a canopy. The other carriage was a full cart, double doors, and from what Mateo could see, leather seating and curtains covering the glass windows. The outside of the carriage had intricate designs carved into the wood. Also, the same "R" crest that was engraved over the balcony was also engraved over the doors on the carriage.

It was very pretty, and Mateo knew that one was for their master, Rama. The driver of the carriage waited by the door, and eventually Rama walked out of his home. He didn't address Mateo or the other men, he only climbed inside of his carriage. The driver closed the door, then walked to the front, taking position and control of the horses' reins.

Cervantes climbed onto the bench of the other carriage with the gladiators and took control of their horse's reins. Soon, both carriages headed out, and Mateo and the other two men were forced to keep pace. They jogged, barely keeping up, and struggled not to fall, lest they be dragged, probably to the arena. They only paused in their journey twice so that the men could rest before moving on.

After an hour of travel, their feet bloody, muscles aching, the men exhausted and mentally, emotionally, and spiritually battered, they finally arrived at the arena. Mateo struggled to catch his breath, but as he did, he looked up at the arena, which was positively magnificent in its appearance. Mateo, mouth agape, stared up at the arena in awe. It was the largest structure he had ever seen. Granted, he hadn't seen much, but what he had seen so far, the arena rivaled all of it. He turned towards the other two men and noticed they were also awestruck by the building.

Nicholas Bella

The arena stood fifteen stories tall and was so wide, it almost looked like a small village to Mateo. The structure was made from marble, stone, and steel, from what he could see, and it was so beautiful with its open windows, carved statues of past gladiators, and the lush greenery that covered some of the walls. He could only imagine what the inside looked like.

He didn't have long to wonder, as the carriages continued forward toward the gladiators' entrance of the arena. Rama's carriage continued on in another direction as theirs stayed on the path. He and the others trotted alongside the carriage Cervantes drove until he stopped once again and disembarked along with the gladiators. Each man climbed out of the carriage, carrying their gear, and stood in a single line. They wore loincloths and sandals, which was different than how they'd all been dressed the night before at the ludus.

Mateo let his eyes wander over the man he was about to face. Haraka stood six-feet-six, a hulking beast with long dread locks that nearly touched his ass. His dark skin was covered in a full body tattoo of tribal markings and other tattoos that Mateo didn't understand. Some were names, and Mateo wondered if those were the names of Haraka's victories, his victims.

"Follow me, filth," Cervantes ordered, and the three prisoners followed behind the doctore, and the gladiators followed behind them, making sure they didn't try to escape, even though that would have been impossible, as Cervantes held tight to their connected chain. The men were led to one room with stone walls and hooks on the wall.

Another man approached Cervantes; he was tall, muscular, and bald. He wore what looked like a linen robe. His blue eyes looked over the three prisoners. "These your offerings? Sad if so, Cervantes."

Cervantes shook his head. "Don't insult, Samson. Not these three, they be filth still needing to prove themselves worthy of the gods in the Trial of Fate. Haraka, Boris, Feilong, Sonder, Osiris, and Titus are our offerings."

Samson's gaze left the three prisoners to look upon the hulking gladiators, and he nodded his approval. "Quite worthy of being offerings, especially the Champion."

"Indeed," Cervantes agreed.

Samson turned back to the three prisoners. "Who will they face?"

Cervantes gestured toward Haraka. "These three must fight him."

Samson nodded. "Ahhh, I see. Do you wish to prepare the gladiators?"

"Aye, but I have these to look after." He nodded his head toward Mateo and the other two men. "I trust you to tend to them."

Samson nodded. "I will take these gladiators and prepare them, then."

Cervantes nodded and gesture for the gladiators to follow the other man. "Go."

The seven gladiators obeyed the command, leaving Cervantes alone with the three prisoners. Normally, the doctore would tend to his men. But regular slaves there to prove themselves worthy of the test were not allowed to go into the gladiator's Hall. So, they remained in the common slave area. Mateo looked around, seeing as they were in this room with two guards and their doctore.

There were three weapons racks along the far wall that contained what looked to be worn and damaged weapons not fit for any battle. The shields were dented and barely usable. It was as if all of the odds were to be stacked against them. Mateo's heart sank even more when he realized that maybe he wasn't supposed to survive this Trial of Fate test.

If that wasn't enough to have on his mind, his stomach growled once more, making him feel nauseated a little. He so desperately wanted food and water, things he'd been in need of the day he had been captured. To keep them alive, he'd been told they'd been given both and stale bread on the ship. Of course, he couldn't remember this, due to his high fever. But that would explain why they were still alive. His thoughts traveled back to his mother and sister, and he hoped they were not starving. Would they still be waiting on his return? Did they know he'd been abducted? Did they think he was still alive?

All of those thoughts captivated his mind and left him even more conflicted about his future. One part of him wanted to give up and just die. The other wanted to fight, so maybe one day, he could see them again. There was always hope.

Cervantes connected their chain to a hook on the wall, ensuring they wouldn't be able to escape at all. Then he turned to address the three. "I will not give you advice. You live if you want to live. You three will fight Haraka at the same time. If you don't survive, you were not worthy. That is all. When your moment comes, weapons will be provided for you, and you make of your fate what you will."

The three men looked at each other, their expressions were of confusion, as not one among them had ever faced a man in combat, especially not to the death. All Mateo knew of were little skirmishes with his childhood friend, Dor, that ended with the adults always breaking them up. Dor passed away four years ago, because living in the badlands was unforgiving and most didn't see forty winters or summers before the harshness of the land took their life.

Now, he would have to give it his all, or die trying. The three prisoners were of the same mind as they each shuffled closer to the entrance leading toward the arena. They were in what one could consider a waiting room. They looked out, spellbound at the grandeur of the arena, which was far more splendid than the outside. Mounted overhead was a huge bracket that held four large screens.

"What are those?" Jorome asked. He'd been the prisoner who'd spoke the most on the way there and who'd had the misfortune of drinking Kodac's piss the night before.

"Screens for closer viewing. The cameras watch what the gladiators do and all of the people get to see," Cervantes informed them, then he snorted. "I bet seeing electricity at work is new to you lot."

He was right, Mateo had never seen such marvels. It both terrified and enchanted him. He stared up at the four screens and felt even more doom. Now everyone would be able to see everything as he fought for his life. On the screens was the crowd, the camera panning over several sections, and when they saw themselves on the screens, the people became even more ecstatic. It all sickened Mateo.

Cervantes kept his watchful eye on the three men, making sure they didn't get away. He watched as they looked out into what may be the place where they'd die. He could see the uncertainty in their gazes, the fear in their bodies as they shook. He didn't think they would survive a bout with Haraka, who was not even in the top ten of their best gladiators. Haraka would be what one could consider a mid-carder. Not championship material, but still entertaining and worthy to shed blood for the gods.

Still, those three prisoners already weaken by hunger would be easy kills for Haraka. And by making their deaths quick, the gods will get their appetite for blood quenched and the better matches of the day could commence. Cervantes smiled to himself as he watched the three men give each other terrified looks. He could hear them discussing what their strategy should be, as if that would help them.

When Cervantes first laid eyes on his master's new slaves, he was not impressed, but then… he rarely was. It took a certain kind of man to give him pause and still be unrefined. If any of these men did survive to be trained, he didn't see any of them rising above mid-carder status.

They just weren't remarkable enough, in his opinion. Well, he paused on the younger one with the pretty brown eyes and full lips. He was a handsome one, and the only regret Cervantes had was that if the boy were to die in the arena, he wouldn't have the opportunity to plunder his mouth and ass with his cock. But it wasn't anything he was dwelling on. His master often rewarded him with female and male beauties for his services. As long as he continued to train some of the best gladiators in the world, he would always be in good favor of not only the gods, but his master.

Mateo leaned against the doorframe as he watched the arena continue to fill with people who came to see men and women die. Who would cheer if or when he fell under Haraka's sword? These people didn't care about the gladiators or their sacrifice. They only cared about being entertained. He hated these people who only wanted bloodshed. He hated the gods who desired it and allowed such atrocities to take place in the name of having a good time.

If this was what the civilized world looked like, Mateo didn't want any part of it. Living in the badlands was hard, but at least they were free and the people didn't kill each other like they did here. The only perk Mateo could see for one living in what was considered the blessed lands was having easy access to food, water, and other necessities. Nothing more.

With every second that passed, Mateo could feel his nerves getting more frazzled. The arena was full of people now and he could see the audience smiling and chatting among themselves, the noise was ominous to him because he knew they would not help him. They would merely be a catalyst to his death. He was appalled as he watched some people even fucking in the stands as if they were animals.

"Won't be much longer now. Once the gods arrive, we can begin," Cervantes said.

The sound of the doctore's voice startled the three men. He'd been so quiet the entire time, they could almost pretend that he wasn't there. Mateo looked at the screen again, seeing it showing the section of the arena that was more luxurious than the rest of it. There was an inset balcony with a blue velvet awning and four ornate, throne-like chairs overlooking the sands. Mateo swallowed hard as he both anticipated and dreaded the arrival of the gods.

For one thing, he'd never seen one. He had only heard the stories of their powers and beauty. He'd also heard the stories of their wrath, which was what he feared the most. These four gods had destroyed the world over two-hundred years ago, killing billions, it was said. The survivors had to rebuild, but only in the way the gods would approve. The celestial cities were huge masses of land on what was called the four corners of the world, and they were connected by the neutral land where the arena resided.

Mateo learned that much on their journey to the arena from one of his fellow prisoners. According to Jorome, the gods lived close to the arena and the people lived close to the gods. Those who lived the closest lived the richest. They helped the gods maintain control. Mateo had seen some of that wealth displayed as they made their way to the arena. Large homes of glass, wood, brick, clay, and stone. Some even had building materials he wasn't familiar with, but Jorome had told him they were rice paper and chrome. There, homes were built on land that required a lot of maintenance and happened to have a lot of security. All of it had mesmerized Mateo and he

40

never knew people lived this way, but he also wondered how much it cost, not in rubios, but in their souls.

He did enjoy the education he was getting, not that he thought it mattered in the long run, seeing as they had been walking to possible doom at the time. The conversation was nice to pass the time away. Jorome didn't come from the same badlands that Mateo had. He was from Sill Delray, one of the badlands in the celestial city of Ocena.

Mateo didn't know if everything Jorome had told him was true, but if it was, he'd learned more about the world around him. His eyes remained glued to those four thrones as if he could will the gods away from them in hopes of extending what little time he had left. Cervantes stepped up beside them, his cold gaze fixed on the thrones as well. Mateo saw him smile out of the corner of his eye and he knew why.

"About time," Cervantes mumbled.

Mateo watched the screen as the four gods took to their respective thrones, each sitting down in a chair that appeared to be the color of their city's flag. The cushions on the goddess Odessa's chair were blue, as was the color of her flag with the waves of the ocean on it. Red was the color of Eloy's throne, and his red flag held the flames. Green for Kijani, as his flag bore the tree with its long roots, and finally white for Simeon, and his white flag featured the artistic lines of wind on it.

Mateo's mouth dropped open as he beheld the four gods in all of their celestial glory. The description of their beauty didn't do them justice. In spite of the distance that separated them, he could still see the muscular and toned bodies of each male god and the soft, curvaceous lines and toned limbs of the delicate female god.

The color of their skin was also different, varying from the ebony tone of Simeon's skin to Kijani whose striking flesh was the color of sand, which was all Mateo could compare it to. Odessa's skin was deeply tanned brown, and Eloy's skin was like Mateo's, tanned as if by the sun's kiss. They each had distinct facial features as well.

The shape of Odessa's eyes were like almonds and Kijani's were similar, but with more of a slant, making him look all the more beautiful and exotic. Simeon's eyes were big, round, and warm, making him look compassionate, whereas Eloy's eyes were narrow, sharp, and cruel... yet beautiful and thoughtful.

Mateo found himself staring at the god of fire, there was just something about the god that he found fascinating. Maybe it was the fact that he seemed to enjoy the atmosphere of the arena more than the other gods, save Odessa, who looked out over the audience with her piercing green gaze in a mixture of contempt and amusement. Eloy's expression was that of pure lust, as if he was getting sexual gratification from the crowd's excitement and his own.

Kijani sat quietly between Odessa and Simeon, and every once in a while, his gaze shifted towards Eloy. Simeon looked to be uninterested all together and Mateo wondered if his assessment was correct. To him, the gods seemed so... human, which was something he hadn't expected. With the power they possessed and the control they had, he was expecting these beings to be like they were in some of the stories he'd been told.

He was expecting the gods to be ten or twelve feet tall with wings and have halos over their heads. Though, he had to admit, their clothing matched the image he had when he imagined what they'd look like. Odessa was wearing a long, ocean-blue silk gown with jeweled straps and halter, and side slits with jeweled clasps. Her ornate crown was made of blue jewels that sparkled brightly in the sun.

Two of the male gods each wore togas made of a shiny material Mateo had never seen before, but it looked like it would be soft if he ever got the chance to touch it. Which he knew he'd never have. Their togas had jeweled clasps and belts that also looked very lavish. Only Eloy was dressed differently. He wore a large gold and jewel necklace, arm and wrist bracelets, and his crotch was covered with a gold loincloth that had red strips of fabric draped over his front and back, leaving his powerful thighs exposed.

He was truly magnificent to behold and Mateo couldn't take his eyes off the god, whose bared, oiled chest made Mateo feel things that awaked his cock. He hadn't really seen a man—correction—god that made his body react that way. Even the gladiators at Rama's ludus, though some were striking, didn't have that effect on him the way the god, Eloy, did.

"The gods," Cervantes said. His voice startled Mateo, who had almost forgotten where he was and what he was there for.

Mateo turned to Cervantes. "Are they as powerful as people say, sir?"

Cervantes nodded. "I have seen them bless us." He turned to the three men. "In all honesty, you are not even worthy to die for them, but my dominus gives them your blood in tribute, so I keep quiet."

Not really that quiet, Mateo thought. Those words cut through him the most, because it was confirmation they'd been brought to the arena solely to die. Something to satisfy the gods, the death of rogues who live in the badlands.

"It has begun," Cervantes said, grinning as he looked out into the arena.

Mateo turned to see the crowd all rise, then drop to one knee, heads bowed to the gods who simply sat there, seeming unimpressed at the worship they were receiving. The four gods raised their right hands, then lowered them, and the crowd as a collective all took their seats. A man dressed in blue linen pants, shirt, and sandals, with a gold sash draped over his left shoulder, stood upon a platform on the second story that overlooked the sands and held something to his mouth that Mateo didn't recognize.

"Welcome to the Day of Champions! We give this day to our beloved gods in our most humbled of worship," the man said through the device he held in his hand, which made his voice boom over the crowd.

"What is that he speaks through, sir?" Mateo asked.

"A microphone. We hear his voice through the speakers," Cervantes replied, though he didn't know why he had. It wasn't like the three prisoners would survive their bout.

"We have quite the offerings for your entertainment. Gladiators from all around have come to shed blood and life for your grace," the announcer said, then he bowed once again to the four gods, who only nodded. "Let us not shed time."

The many people in the crowd cheered and laughed at what Mateo concluded was a joke, though he was not laughing. He was far too nervous to feel anything but gut-wrenching fear. His palms were sweating and his stomach was doing flip-flops as the seconds ticked by.

"Before the real matches begin, let us give gratitude to the Honorable Aurelius Turetto, Chairman of the High Senate, for sponsoring this Game."

The crowd cheered as an older man with short-cropped, white hair and a white Sherwani suit with gold trim stood for the audience to acknowledge him. He bowed to the gods, waved to the crowd, and then sat back down.

The announcer continued. "Dominus Rama has three prisoners from the badlands to put on display for the pleasure of the gods. They will face off with his gladiator, Haraka."

The crowd erupted into cheers as they anticipated any bloodshed.

"If the three survive the Trial of Fate and receive the favor of the gods, Rama will train them to become full gladiators who will, no doubt, give this arena and his ludus much glory," the announcer boasted to the cheers of the crowd.

"Begin it!" Eloy yelled out, as he had grown impatient with the pomp and circumstance after hearing about the Trial of Fate.

"Yes, God Eloy, of course," the announcer said, then he held up his hand and brought it down. "Begin!"

With that one word, Mateo felt his heart leap into his throat. He probably would have vomited had he had food in his stomach to bring up. Cervantes unhooked their chains that kept them connected, then removed his sword from its sheath.

"Go or face certain death here," he ordered as he aimed his blade at their throats.

The three men knew they had no choice but to face their fate, whatever it was. They walked out into the arena with the bright light of the sun beaming down on them. The crowd booed them and threw rotten fruit and vegetables at them, which pelted their bodies, leaving foul smelling juices and pulp dripping down their flesh. They tried to ignore the crowd as they walked towards the three battered swords that lay in the sand.

Mateo picked one up, as did the other two men. He felt the heftiness in his hand, trying to feel the balance. He looked at the dull, jagged blade and swallowed hard as he noted the disadvantage they'd been given. *Was this really about to happen?* He'd never held a sword before, but was quite handy with a knife. Unfortunately, he didn't have one at the moment. He'd brought down a few pigs with a knife before. He was going to have to apply those skills to this fight. The disappointed roar of the crowd shifted to rabid cheers when Haraka entered the arena.

Again, Mateo felt his body stiffen with terror as the menacing gladiator approached them with a stride that was full of confidence. His torso was covered with a brown leather chest plate for armor, bearing the crest of Rama. Both wrists and shins were also covered with leather for protection. None of which Mateo and the other men had. Haraka gripped his sword tightly in his hand and held his strong bronze shield in the other. Mateo could see the gladiator's eyes trained on them behind his bronze helmet, which completely covered the man's head.

"Oh shit," Marcus said, and Mateo turned to him in time to see the puddle of urine forming beneath the man's feet as it streamed down his leg.

"Remember, we work together, we have chance," Jorome said as he gripped the hilt of his sword.

Mateo's mouth went completely dry as the roar of the crowd hit a new crescendo just as Haraka raised his blade towards him. As if on instinct, he raised his sword, blocking the first strike. Haraka stepped backward, pulling his sword back and thrusting forward, stabbing Mateo in his side, since he was not fast enough to block the second blow.

Mateo cried out as blood gushed from his wound and ran in rivulets down his leg. Haraka pulled the blade from his side and swung, but Mateo dodged the blow as he lunged to the side, gripping his wound. The other prisoners each attacked Haraka, hacking and slashing with their swords, trying their best to stay alive and kill the gladiator.

Mateo looked down at the gaping, bleeding hole in his abdomen. Was this his end? To bleed out in an arena as people cheered? And they were cheering. He looked up to see Haraka kick Jorome to the sands and slash at Marcus, cutting off his hand. Blood spurted from the wound as Marcus looked on in shock at his severed limb. Haraka grunted as he reared back and swung, slicing his blade through Marcus' neck, separating his head from his body.

More blood rained down upon the sands as Marcus' body collapsed to the ground, to the delight of the crowd who demanded more. Mateo looked around in horror, watching as thousands cried for their deaths, and he steeled himself from it all, blocking it out. He had to live, had to survive this test, this moment in time.

Jorome regained his footing and took his best defensive position against Haraka, who stalked towards him, the blade of his sword dripping blood on the sands as he approached the man. Mateo knew he couldn't lay there and die. He wouldn't die for their entertainment. Damn them! Damn them all! He growled as he struggled to get to his feet. He stumbled towards Haraka, pitting the gladiator between himself and Jorome. He swung his sword, but his blade was blocked by Haraka's sword as Jorome's blade was blocked by the gladiator's shield.

They didn't give up; both men continued to slice, hack, and swing at Haraka, hoping one of their blows would make contact. With every cut, nick, and slice their blades claimed on Haraka's flesh, Mateo gained more confidence that he might survive. The crowd seem to grow in its excitement as the battle raged on longer than any of them had expected. Could these two prisoners actually win?

CHAPTER SIX

Eloy leaned forward as he watched the fight wage on. At first, he wasn't too impressed with the three men who'd entered the arena, granted, one did catch his eye. The prettiest of the lot, but he knew he'd be dead in a matter of seconds once the real gladiator joined the party. Never did he expect to see such vigor in the young man who, even injured, was fighting with so much passion. He wanted to live, and watching the boy struggle against a man who was his better thrilled Eloy.

"Does the god, Eloy, see something he likes?" Odessa asked him.

"Possibly," was Eloy's one word response as his eyes remained glued to the pretty young one whose body looked like it wanted to give up, but his heart and mind wouldn't let it.

"They should both surrender and let the gladiator take them. It would be a more merciful death," Simeon said.

"Giving up is not in this boy's future," Eloy said. "Besides, what is the fun in that?"

"He'll die, it's only a matter of time," Kijani grumbled. He frowned as he watched the humans battle it out. Again, he cut a glance over to Eloy and his frown deepened as he watched his fellow god be transfixed by the one human on the sands. He wanted the boy to die if only to take Eloy's attention away from him.

Eloy gripped the armrest of his throne as Mateo was slashed across his chest by Haraka's blade. The boy's blood flowed from the wound as he fell down to one knee. He bit his bottom lip as Mateo rolled out of the way just as Haraka brought his sword down. The other prisoner charged toward the gladiator, his blade held high above head.

Eloy saw the error in attacking this way, and it came to fruition when Haraka blocked the man's sword with his shield and ran the man through his chest with his sword. The crowd erupted in applause and cheers with two men dead and one to go.

Haraka pulled his blade from Jorome's corpse and turned all of his attention on Mateo. Though he had dominated the fight, he hadn't remained unscathed, as the three prisoners managed to cut and slice him on both arms, legs, and on his chest. The wounds ranged from shallow to deep, requiring stitches. He stalked over to Mateo who was scooting back, trying to regroup. His sword dripped with the blood and flesh of his victims and he smiled behind the mask as he drew closer to his last.

Eloy's heart pounded in his chest as he saw the desperation to survive in Mateo's eyes. It was a look he'd become accustomed to seeing in many eyes, but there was something about the boy's fight for life that spoke to him. The sand was covered in puddles of blood from the four men in the arena and still the crowd screamed for more. And their fervor fed into Eloy's own bloodlust, only he wanted the boy to win.

Mateo managed to climb to his feet, his body weakened from lack of nutrition and blood at this point. This would be his final stand, he would not die on his feet cowering. Haraka blocked his sword with his shield and thrust forward, causing him to fall back, his body hitting the sand hard. He grunted in pain and rolled away from the threat that thirsted for his life. Haraka was on him again, not giving him a chance to get his bearings before he brought the blade down once more.

Mateo blocked it with his sword, but then Haraka kicked his bleeding wound, causing Mateo to double over in excruciating pain. Standing over him, Haraka raised his blade and brought it down to deliver the final blow. Mateo's eyes widened, his heart thundered in his chest, and his breathing ceased as he saw his death approaching.

"Stop!" Eloy commanded, the power in his voice silencing the crowd and stilling Haraka's hand, stopping the blade inches from Mateo's throat.

Odessa chuckled. "It would seem that the god, Eloy, has eyes for the human," she teased.

"Why bother? Let him die, he isn't worthy," Kijani complained, the frown on his face deepening.

"Will you give him your blessing?" Simeon asked Eloy. The fact that his fellow god had interceded had him quite intrigued, as it was a first.

Eloy ignored the chatter from the other gods and raised his hand, officially halting the match. Haraka lowered his weapon and bowed his head, then took a few steps away from Mateo, who was looking around in a state of confusion.

"This one outlasted the others who were not worthy, and he fought bravely. I will see him on these sands again, as a trained gladiator," Eloy said, then lowered his hand to the cheer of the crowd.

"Ahh, so the god, Eloy, grants this human his favor. This one does not wonder why as she can see the lust in the god, Eloy's, eyes when he looks at that battered human," Odessa crooned, grinning.

"He has earned the privilege to fight again, is all," Eloy said as he settled back into his throne. His eyes didn't leave Mateo as the young man struggled to rise to his feet with Haraka's help. The two walked off the sands as the crowd cheered.

"Should have let him die," Kijani grumbled. "The wretch didn't even give you gratitude for sparing his pathetic life. That alone warrants his death."

"Mercy is always a thing we should grant," Simeon countered.

"Bah!" Kijani scoffed and waved his hand dismissively at Simeon, who only gave him a knowing smirk.

"Besides, he was so wounded. When he is healed, if he survives his injuries, I'm sure he'll show his gratitude," Simeon added.

Kijani turned his gaze from Simeon to Eloy, and his eyes narrowed as he speculated the real reason why Eloy wanted to spare the human. It sickened him, Eloy's rampant desires to bed these humans when none of them were worthy to touch the flesh of a god, in his opinion.

"I look forward to more matches," Eloy said, then gestured for the announcer to continue the day's events. As far as he was concerned, the gladiatorial matches started off with such promise.

Mateo's body burned like fire where he'd been sliced and stabbed. He could barely walk and leaned all of his weight on Haraka, who was talking to him as they both limped back to Cervantes.

"You are very fortunate that a god blessed you. Even I do not know why," Haraka said. "I doubt you survive the training it takes to be a gladiator, but remember this day."

Mateo heard the words spoken to him, but couldn't really concentrate on their meaning as he was still reeling from having lasted the battle. Granted, it was not on his own skill, for he had none, and Haraka proved that in the arena. He was surprised he had endured as long as he had and he knew part of that was because of the other two men he'd fought with. The other part was because he didn't want to die.

Up until the moment when he was finally out there on the sands, he'd been going back and forth in his mind over whether or not he should give up and die to free himself of an uncertain hellish future or fight for whatever future he did have. It wasn't until Haraka's blade had clashed with his that his decision became final.

Haraka brought him into the waiting area where Cervantes was still shaking his head in bewilderment. Mateo was placed on the bench and he held his hand over the most severe wound he had, which was the wound in his abdomen.

"Never have I seen the gods bless one so low," Cervantes said as he stood over Mateo.

"Neither have I," said a voice from behind them, and the three men each turned to see Rama enter in through the second entrance. "Have Kodac see to him, make sure he does not die. Bathe him and feed him. I will stay behind with my other gladiators until you return."

Cervantes nodded. "Yes, dominus." He turned to Haraka. "Bring him."

Haraka grunted in response and scooped up Mateo's beaten and starved body, carrying it out of the arena and towards their carriage. While en route back to their home and the medicus,

Cervantes applied what first aid he knew to stop the bleeding and help kill infection. Mateo could only lay still as the doctore tended to his wounds. The one thing he was grateful for, besides being alive still, was that he didn't have to walk home.

When they finally arrived back at the ludus, he was carried from the carriage to another room inside the main house. He tried to take in his surroundings, but his vision was blurring in and out and he couldn't make sense of the things he was seeing or hearing. He knew he was being placed on a surface that was the softest he'd felt since being kidnapped.

It didn't take too much longer, not with this new comfort, for him to completely lose consciousness, and he welcomed it. When Mateo woke up, the room was dim and lit only by a few candles. When he attempted to sit up, the pain in his muscles and the sting of his wounds forced him to lie back down.

"Take it easy," a sweet, female voice said, then she approached him and he could see who was talking. She was pretty, blonde, with gray eyes and soft, bow-shaped lips that made her look like a doll his sister once had. She didn't look to be older than fifteen and the soft cadence of her voice was comforting as she spoke to him. "You suffered greatly in the arena and have many wounds. But are strong."

"I... I can't believe I still live," Mateo said as he thought back to the moment in the arena when he'd seen his life flash before his eyes. Haraka was standing over him, blade raised high and poised to deliver the final blow until a bellowing voice called out to him over the hush of the crowd.

It was all coming back to him, and he was amazed that he'd been spared by a god. They really did give their blessings to those who they felt were worthy. But what made him more worthy than the two men who had died by his side? Why were they not spared their fate?

"Why was I spared?" he asked the young lady.

She shrugged. "No one knows. The gods rarely spare lives, and those are only of the gladiators. Never a slave like you or me."

"Are gladiators not slaves, too?" Mateo asked.

The girl looked off to the side. "They are, but of the highest quality as they give their lives to the gods. Their sacrifices can elevate the house of their dominus, and their victories can save their cities if they continue to gain the gods' favor. Today, you have done such." She reached behind his head, raising it ever so slightly. "Here, drink. You need nourishment."

Mateo greedily drank the broth the girl fed him, only slowing down when she forced him to pause between his gulps. He was so hungry that had he had the strength, he would have snatched the bowl from her and devoured every last drop. But, he was weak and needed her assistance, so he took small sips like she instructed until the broth was all gone. He licked his lips, trying to get every taste he could as it was the best thing he'd eaten in days.

"Your stomach may reject it, then it may not. We start with broth until you can take solids," she explained. "Rest now." She placed a cool cloth over his forehead, which Mateo relished as it seemed to soothe so many of his aliments. His stomach was still growling and he wanted more broth, but the girl had advised against it, lest he purge everything he'd eaten.

He took her advice and rested. Every once in a while, he'd wake up to the sound of men talking. The last time the voices woke him, he turned to see a gladiator sitting on one of the beds with whom he assumed was the medicus examining him.

"You are healing well," the medicus said.

"When will I be able to take to the sands again?" the gladiator asked.

The medicus grumbled. "So eager to die, are you?"

"Eager to see this house raised in the eyes of the gods and to see myself blessed and freed, yes," the gladiator said.

The medicus sighed. "Not for at least a month. Your injury was deep, too deep for such a quick recovery. You must give your body time to heal or you will see death the next time you take to the sands."

To that, the gladiator groaned and frowned. "A month when I will be unable to train. A full month when I must miss the next Games."

The medicus shrugged. "Next time, dodge your opponent's blow." He finished wrapping the wound and took a step back. "There. Now rest."

The gladiator mumbled something else, though Mateo didn't hear what he said, but by the chuckle coming from the medicus, apparently he had, and hadn't taken any offense to it. The gladiator looked at Mateo and his frowned deepened.

"What makes you so special?" he asked.

Mateo didn't bother to respond because he didn't have an answer. He also didn't want to take what felt like a baiting taunt, and with both of them injured, neither could risk coming to blows.

"Balls and cocks, Osiris, let the boy alone. Go rest now," the medicus ordered, shooing the other man out of the room. He then turned his attention back to Mateo.

"We all would like to know what makes you so special that one of the most volatile gods saw fit to spare your life. Perhaps your life was not so worthless after all. Now, we just need to see just how much your life is worth," a voice said, and Mateo recognized it as Rama's.

Mateo turned to see his dominus walking toward him.

"He is doing well, dominus," the medicus said.

"How well?" Rama asked.

"His fever is gone, finally. He's been able to hold down food, so we have moved from broth to soup. His wounds are healing very well, dominus. The scars should be barely visible," the medicus said.

Rama waved his hand dismissively. "I care not about his scars. For a gladiator, they are the trophies of his victories. He should regard them as such… that is if he ever sees the sands again. There is still his training. When can that begin?"

"Not for at least two months, dominus. That is if you really want him to have a fair chance."

Rama groaned. "He will have a month. I need to see what the god, Eloy, saw in this boy."

"Apologies, dominus, but I must insist. You risk entering a gladiator into the Games who is not fully healed. It would only lead to a poor showing and the gods will be angered," the medicus warned.

Rama groaned as he pondered that predicament. "Kijani's cock! What herbs do you need to hasten his healing as well as Osiris'?"

"Wickleberry is the best. I can make a paste and juice from it. That will hasten the healing," the medicus said.

"I will have some acquired." Rama looked at Mateo. "Tell me, boy, what is your name?"

So much had happened to Mateo, he had completely forgotten that these men who had decided his fate didn't even know his name, nor did they seem to care before.

"Mateo, dominus," Mateo replied.

Rama nodded. "Mateo... I suppose I could let you keep that name. It is a good, strong name, worthy of a gladiator. You will begin your training in three weeks. Take care of yourself so you can survive. You will be trained in the style of Sakata."

Mateo sat up a little, bracing himself on his elbows as he looked at Rama. "What is that, dominus?"

"With your body type, I think it's best you learn to master the katana and wakizashi... a short sword," Rama added when he saw the confusion on Mateo's face. "Of course, your body will be put through physical training, as I want you to bulk up. I watched you in that arena, you are agile, and that is good."

"That style will suit him well, dominus," the medicus agreed.

"It will. Now, the god, Eloy, spared you, even though he is known to be unforgiving of failure, yet he saved you from your own as you could not best Haraka. Perhaps while you heal, we can appease Eloy in other ways," Rama said, then he took a few more steps closer to Mateo. "Are you virgin?"

Mateo blinked several times, having been taken aback by the boldness of the question. Such things just weren't asked of people so openly in the badlands. The longer Mateo was exposed to this so-called civilized society, the more *they* seemed like the wildlings they claim *them* to be.

"Yes, dominus," Mateo answered truthfully. He was only nineteen, and though he had feelings for other men, he had never once indulged in them.

Rama smirked. "Let's see if you speak truth." He slipped his hand between Mateo's thighs and Mateo tried to shove Rama's hand away, but was rewarded with a backhanded slap across his face, which laid him out flat on the bed. "Filth! You belong to me. Never seek to refuse me again. Comprehend?"

Mateo caressed his cheek where the newly forming bruise stung. "Yes, dominus, apologies."

"You think because a god granted you his favor that you don't belong to me?" Rama growled. His cruel gray eyes bored into Mateo's brown, conveying his rage at being checked by his own slave.

Mateo shook his head. "No, dominus."

"Good. I will do with your body what I wish and you will obey. The only free will you have is what I give you, comprehend?" Rama's cold gaze bored into Mateo, demanding his obedience.

Mateo nodded. "Yes, dominus."

Rama, now satisfied with his slave's answers, continued to slide his hand between Mateo's legs. "Open wider."

Mateo tried to keep calm, for he'd never had anyone touch him so intimately before. Even when he had been with the bandits and on that stage, strange fingers hadn't gone where Rama's fingers were going now. He felt his master probe his anal passage and winced as the tip of the finger breached his opening.

"Ooohh, that is lovely. Fresh and untouched. So tight, I almost want to enjoy taking you myself, but I will save you for the god, Eloy. Yes, that shall please him greatly, for when was the last time he's had a virgin?" Rama speculated as he smiled devilishly, thinking about how much fortune his house would get if he could make Mateo something a god would desire.

"For such activity, dominus, may I suggest three more weeks of healing?" the medicus asked.

"Two weeks. He can simply lay still," Rama stated.

"That he can, dominus, but may we consider that the god, Eloy, may not desire such inactivity?"

Again, Rama groaned in annoyance that he couldn't get his way because his medicus continued to advise against it. "Fine. Three weeks. Make sure he is ready to please the god then."

"Yes, dominus," the medicus said.

Mateo wasn't as worldly as the other men he'd been imprisoned with, but he knew damn well what was being discussed in front of him and about him as if he wasn't there. He knew he didn't have a say in the matter either, which enraged him. They would give him to the god, Eloy, to sate his sexual desires with his body. The thought made him want to rage out and attack everyone in the room, but he didn't have the full strength of his body yet... or even the physical skill to pull off such an attack.

Never before had he felt so helpless. Still, he didn't regret being alive, because there was always hope. He was never without hope.

CHAPTER SEVEN

Eloy leaned his head back as he sat in his throne enjoying the oral pleasures of one of his six male slaves. The way the slave's mouth enveloped his cock sent tingles down his spine and he groaned in ecstasy. The slave's fingers coaxed more sensation from his cock, making his nearing climax all the more intense.

"Hurry up and cum so that we can hold a normal conversation," Simeon fussed as he sat in the opposite throne, legs crossed and arms resting on the armrest.

"Don't rush me…ahhhh," Eloy retorted.

Simeon sighed deeply, clearly displaying his annoyance. "You invited me over."

"You invited yourself," Eloy corrected.

"You made it seem as though you wanted the company when I called," Simeon countered.

"I do." Annoyed, Eloy opened his eyes and looked at his fellow god. "Why don't you enjoy the pleasures of one of my slaves, then? They have been expertly trained." He gestured to one of the males standing by, wearing nothing but a sheer golden loincloth that concealed nothing as the male's genitalia was still visible. But that was the way Eloy liked it.

Simeon casted a disinterested look towards the slave, then huffed. "I'm not horny, which unfortunately for me, you seem to be at all times."

Eloy smirked. "Pity for you." He closed his eyes and leaned his head back once again, giving himself to the sexual skills of his slave.

Simeon rolled his eyes and rose from the throne, making his way towards the balcony. He stepped out onto it, enjoying the gentle, cool breeze that he was responsible for. He rarely denied the humans such a luxury as wind, but when he was out voted by his fellow gods, he agreed to deal out the punishment they wanted. If the humans failed to worship them properly, especially at the Games, then they took turns, alternating between punishments. On such occasions, he might take the breeze away, leaving the air stagnant and sweltering in some areas or blistering and freezing in others.

Still, it was nothing compared to what Kijani would do if he felt slighted by the race he deemed inferior. The god of earth was well known to create deadly earthquakes on massive scales, and in some places, make the soil so dry, nothing would grow. That, of course, was in conjunction with the goddess Odessa who would simply deny the humans water. That meant no rain, and she could hold that off indefinitely if she so chose to.

Much worse was making the lands flood, which was something Odessa had done in the past, which claimed many lives, crops, and damaged a great deal. The people did not deny that the gods were real, but they were feared more than loved. This much Simeon understood and loathed. Unfortunately, he seemed to be the only one among his fellow gods that missed the adoration, as the other three seemed to be satisfied with being the menace the humans bowed to in terror, rather than truly worshipped out of respect.

When he heard Eloy's loud moans, he knew his fellow god had hit his climax and would be more engaged for a conversation. He waited a few minutes, letting Eloy tend to his needs, then he entered the living room again just as Eloy was dismissing all of his slaves.

"Finally," Simeon commented as he took a seat in the throne chair again.

Eloy chuckled. "Really, my friend, I don't understand your distaste."

Simeon waved his hand dismissively. "Not distaste. I have enjoyed the pleasure this flesh yields over the many decades. However, you and Odessa's rampant desires surpasses my own."

Eloy shrugged, as it was quite true. It was as if he could not get enough sex and had to have it daily. His body's endurance was heighted over any human's, but he could still be drained of energy. It was then that he would feel sexually satisfied. He really didn't understand why Kijani and Simeon didn't have similar desires.

"So, have you spoken to Kijani recently?" Simeon asked.

"Argh, I'd rather not."

Simeon chuckled. "He is still cross with you for interfering with the fight at the Games."

"Three weeks have passed and he still holds an unnecessary grudge," Eloy mumbled.

"His lust for you makes his grudge very necessary. You know he doesn't like when your interest wanders from him," Simeon pointed out.

"If only he had just cause."

"You've bedded each other. That is just cause enough for Kijani."

Eloy chuckled. "And it's *my* temper that gets called into question."

Simeon arched an eyebrow. "Ah, but your temper is as fiery as your power, Eloy. I must be honest, even I am curious as to why you halted the fight. Were not the other two prisoners worthy of your mercy?"

"No, they were not," Eloy replied.

"Then, what makes this one human stand above the rest?"

"He fascinates me."

"And no others have before him?"

"None."

"I know of one who did," Simeon stated with a knowing smirk.

Eloy cocked an eyebrow. "And only you know of him. Keep it that way."

"No point in saying anything now. That was decades ago. Besides, it would only enrage Kijani for no reason," Simeon said, and then laughed.

"He died too young," Eloy whispered softly as he thought back to the one human who'd captured his heart.

"He did, but it was for the best."

Eloy snarled at Simeon. "Be careful how you speak."

Simeon raised his hand, calming Eloy's temper. "I say that not to offend, but to remind. We agreed to never take a human lover.

It is forbidden. Their lifespans are but a blink of an eye compared to us. To take one would only cause a war as jealousies mounted."

Eloy sighed. "All this I know."

"And yet, eighty years ago, you ignored."

"That was eighty years ago, Simeon."

"Very well," the god of wind conceded... somewhat. "I just feel concern as you've shown favor among one from the least impressive lifeforms... according to Kijani and Odessa."

"And why do you take interest in what has captured my attention?" Eloy asked, leaning forward a little.

"Because very little interests you beyond quenching your desires. Is that what you want? To sink your cock into that human? I'd understand if that was it. He was fetching... or is it something more?"

Eloy thought about what he wanted from that human whose name he still did not know. He had been captivated by the boy's struggle to survive against a foe who was destined and more than capable to end him. There was something about the boy that spoke to Eloy, but he wasn't quite sure what it was. Apart from that mystery feeling, he did desire the boy and wanted to feel his flesh buried deeply inside the boy's hot, tight, passage.

He looked at Simeon, smiling. "You know me well, my friend. Most males as pretty as he is are destined for the brothels. I am interested to see what kind of warrior he will become."

"And you are intended to have him in your bed?" Simeon asked.

"Oh, indeed," Eloy admitted.

"Well, that clears it up for me. Although, I'm sure such reasons will not appease Kijani."

"Kijani wishes to have me all to himself simply because we did bed before. He will simply have to accept that he will not," Eloy said, then he slapped his knee. "I could not interest you in my slaves, but would you also refuse the delicacies of my chefs?"

"Ah!" Simeon placed his hand over his stomach and grinned widely. "Now, that is the way to my heart."

Eloy laughed, then rose from his throne and walked towards the door, opening it. "We will dine now."

"Yes, God Eloy." The human slave bowed his head and ran off to fetch the food.

Eloy returned to his throne and waited for the food to arrive, which it did on several silver platters. Those closest to where the gods lived could enjoy the luxuries of being so blessed, which was finer clothing, dwellings, running water, electricity, and delicious food. The further one lived, the more those luxuries became basic or non-existent. Just one of the reasons why humans did what they could to stay close and keep the gods happy.

Eloy indulged in the roasted rosemary chicken, potatoes, fruit, and vegetables that his chef had prepared and Simeon partook as well. The two gods discussed random topics, nothing too revealing around the human servants who held the silver platters of which they dined upon.

Another servant entered the room, walking over to Eloy, and bowed as he presented an envelope. "God Eloy, this letter just arrived for you."

Eloy sucked the juices from his fingertips and took the letter, then waved away the servant, who left without saying a word. Eloy read who the letter came from and smirked.

"Good news, I take it?" Simeon speculated as he devoured his roasted chicken. Human food was something he'd never get tired of enjoying. There was always so many ways to prepare a meal and so many delights to sample. If he had one weakness, one sin he'd fallen victim to that he'd admit, it was gluttony.

"Possibly," Eloy said as he opened the letter and read its contents. A slow smile spread across his lips as he read what the letter offered him. Something he'd hadn't had the opportunity to enjoy in quite some time.

"That smile of yours makes me more curious," Simeon said, eyeing his friend suspiciously.

Eloy looked up at him. "Be curious, then." He placed the envelope in the cushions of his throne. "This business is my own." He gestured for the human servant to lower the platter containing the rest of his chicken and he broke off a leg, then took a generous bite.

"So be it," Simeon said, not willing to press, although he could guess what the letter said by the smile on Eloy's face. Probably an invitation to a new brothel, as Eloy seemed to enjoy those almost as much as he enjoyed the monthly Games.

The two gods soon parted as the hours became too late and both gods felt the exhaustion take their bodies. Being all powerful was one thing, but being inside a mortal casing meant that they were also subjected to human vulnerabilities. Eloy climbed into his huge bed and pondered what he would do with such an offering.

The human who he'd spared was also untouched. His body pure, and he was being offered the chance to pluck his flower, and rightfully so. As far as he was concerned, no human should be allowed to take one's virginity, as such privilege was reserved for the divine. Unfortunately, many humans had already been deflowered prior to sharing his bed, as brothels or other humans took the advantage. It was a disappointment he'd grown accustomed to, which was why such an occasion as this was a rarity, and one he'd enjoy.

Had Eloy found out that the boy whose name he'd just learned from the letter was Mateo, had lost his virginity to one of them, he would have been most displeased. Most displeased. It never ceased to amaze him that most humans risked their wrath by not giving their virgins over to them and instead, took the pleasure for themselves. Of course, there was the fact that only he and Odessa desired the sexual company of humans, as Kijani didn't touch humans and Simeon could give or take them. When they weren't unified on an issue, then they could not bring it into law.

Another thing that came into play was the High Senate and Elite Security of Defense officials. They were the exception, as well as ludus and brothel owners. It was one perk given to those who served the gods well. But it also meant that Eloy and Odessa often didn't get to have virgins.

Mateo would be a real treat. He had plans to have the boy brought to his home, where he would sate his desires with the virgin before sending him back to his dominus. Just the thought of sinking his cock deep into the tight, virginal hole of the beautiful male sent blood surging to Eloy's cock, hardening it. He summoned one of his male servants to tend to his new erection.

The human entered the room, kneeling to Eloy. "My god, what do you want of me?"

"Pleasure my cock," Eloy commanded, and the man nodded as he rose.

Eloy's amber eyes watched as the human climbed into the bed and straddled his lap. The human was pretty with slender limbs and defined abs. He kept his blue-eyed gaze cast downward to avoid Eloy's. The servant leaned over, taking up the sensual oil on the nightstand and pouring a nice amount over Eloy's massive twelve-inch cock.

Eloy moaned as the human stroked his meat, slicking it up with the oil. "Enough teasing, boy." Of course that boy's name was Lane, but Eloy rarely referred to his human servants by their names.

"Yes, God Eloy," the servant said. He'd been a servant in Eloy's house since he was fourteen. Now twenty, he knew exactly what Eloy enjoyed and what he didn't. He raised up high enough to mount Eloy's huge member, then slid down slowly. He had to brace himself for the stretching that it took in order to fully bottom out on Eloy's shaft.

"Ahhhh, yes," Eloy purred as he succumbed to the pleasure of his servant's ass. He'd been with women before as well, and though their bodies offered a different kind of pleasure for his cock, he preferred the sensation of male flesh pressed against his.

The servant rocked his hips back and forth as he bounced up and down, making sure to please the god whose cock he was riding. No one wanted to face Eloy's wrath if he wasn't satisfied. One servant who'd failed to pleasure the god found himself tossed to lions in the arena for the entertainment of the crowd. Eloy himself had cheered the man's gruesome death, and that knowledge was burned into the minds of those who served him.

Eloy gripped the servant's hips as he pumped up, meeting flesh with flesh until his balls drew up. The servant's moans grew louder and his body tensed as they both neared their climaxes.

"Please... oh please, may I cum on you, God Eloy?" the servant begged.

Eloy looked at the boy's rigid dick, red at the tip and dripping precum onto his stomach. He enjoyed it when the humans spent their loads over his body, but he still wanted them to ask for his permission.

"Cum for me," he commanded. His grip on the servant's hips tightened as his own orgasm rushed through his body.

The servant threw his head back, crying out in sheer ecstasy as his cock fired off several wads of thick, creamy seed all over Eloy's abs and pecs. The sight sent Eloy over the edge and he filled the servant with his thick and plentiful load. His body tensed, muscles straining as he bit his bottom lip while enjoying the pleasure of his release. The god of life was on to something when he made sex feel this good.

Eloy jerked a few times until he shuddered as the last of his seed squirted from his slit into Lane's ass. Finally sated, he slapped the servant's ass, which meant he wanted the slave to get off him, and the male quickly obeyed.

"Shall I bathe you, God Eloy?" the servant asked as his gaze looked at the seed drying on Eloy's torso.

Eloy looked down and chuckled. "Lick it off."

The servant smiled and leaned down, licking his cum from the god's golden, muscular chest. Eloy watched as the boy's pink tongue lapped up all the pearly whiteness from his flesh. He liked the way it felt to be licked all over his body. At times, he'd demand full tongue baths and could reach climax just from that alone.

"Good, now go," he ordered once the servant was finished.

"Yes, God Eloy," the servant said, then immediately left the room.

This time, Eloy didn't think about Mateo. He was far too relaxed and satisfied to think about sex. Now, all he wanted was sleep.

CHAPTER EIGHT

Mateo knew of the letter that Rama had sent to the god, Eloy, offering his body for the god's pleasure. He also knew there was nothing he could say or do about it. For the three weeks that he spent healing from his injuries, he was to remain untouched. Several gladiators had been punished for having attempted to take him for themselves, and it was no secret now that he was a virgin.

That knowledge alone seemed to excite and enrage the other gladiators who wanted him. As a precaution, he slept in a cell alone, which was far nicer than the first cell he'd been tossed into. This one at least had some comfort and a bucket to piss in. He was tended to by several female servants and the medicus. The Wickleberry medicine they had given to him was healing him even faster than they had anticipated and that pleased Rama, who had plans for Mateo.

Mateo sat in his cage watching the gladiators as they bathed after their rigorous day and night of training. He listened as they insulted and jested with each other. There were a few who were fucking in the corner in front of everyone and no one seemed to care. That kind of display was something Mateo wasn't used to. People in the badlands were more modest and kept such intimate interaction away from prying eyes.

One of the gladiators walked up to his cell and he leaned back as the man shoved his fat, dirty cock through the bars. "Suck it," he ordered.

The man was one that frightened Mateo. His body was covered in scars from his time in the arena, which meant he was a seasoned gladiator. His muscles were massive and extremely defined, and he stood over six-foot-four, from what Mateo could guess. The man's black hair was cut in a Mohawk and his beard was thick and wild.

The gladiator's gray eyes stared down at Mateo. "You heard me, little fox… your mouth isn't virgin like your cunt. Suck it!" He wiggled his uncut cock at Mateo, who scooted back from the bars.

"You're not supposed to do that," Mateo warned.

"Shut your mouth, you fucking whore!" the gladiator spat at Mateo, hitting him on his cheek.

Mateo jerked back, hitting the wall behind him. He wanted to wipe the spit away immediately, but he didn't want the gladiator to know it affected him, so he didn't. "Get away from me," he snarled. Though he feared the man, he would never let him know it. So, he kept his expression hard as he glared back in his resolution.

"I'll fuck you soon enough after your cherry cunt gets busted in," he snarled, and then walked away, back towards the others. Some of the men laughed at his antics.

"Boris, you frighten the little bird," one of the other gladiators said as he slapped Boris on his back.

"I'll break that little bird's wings, too," Boris added as he looked back at Mateo and blew a kiss at him, taunting Mateo further.

Well, at least Mateo knew the man's name. Boris. He groaned as he wiped Boris' stinking saliva from his face and cleaned his hand off on his loincloth. He'd seen men be boorish in the badlands, but they were easy enough to avoid and tended to hang out in one area. But even still, they weren't on this level of barbarism. He laid down on the thin, flimsy mattress that was provided to him so he wouldn't have to sleep on the floor, but only because he was healing. The other gladiators had let him know that the floor was where he would have been sleeping had he not been injured. But then again, some reminded him that he wouldn't even have to worry about where he'd be sleeping had the god of fire not called an end to the match.

It'd been three weeks since that fateful day when his life changed once again and was given new meaning. Of course, he had no way of knowing how much longer his life would last considering he was to be trained as a gladiator, whose sole purpose was to fight to the death all of the damned time. He had asked one of the nicer men, Malec, a few questions because he seemed to be more inclined to not treat him like the others did.

He wanted to know if any other gladiator had actually earned their freedom, and the answer was yes. After many battles and glory given to the gods and the house he or she served, seven gladiators had been set free. Their dominus, Rama, being one of the lucky few. The number was hopeful to Mateo, but not by much. The gladiatorial matches had been taking place for over a hundred years with monthly Games. Out of all of that time, only seven gladiators had earned their freedom. Would he be so bold as to think he'd make eight?

Another question he'd asked was if surviving the training would be possible and Malec had told him only if he wanted it bad enough. Of course, that made sense to Mateo. He wanted it, and with the knowledge of a gladiator being set free, he had something to fight for, as did the rest of them. Although, Mateo sensed that some of the men only wanted to fight for glory, and even a death in the arena was an honorable and welcomed one.

Mateo didn't share those sentiments and maybe he never would. A loud bang against his cell bars jarred him from his thoughts and he lifted his head to see who'd disturbed him.

"Dominus wishes to see you," Cervantes informed him, then proceeded to open the door.

Mateo rose from the mattress and made his way over to his doctore. Once the door was opened, he walked through and was accompanied by both Cervantes and another guard. There were at least ten guards on the premises from what Mateo could see, but that wasn't to say there weren't more. His access to the main house was limited.

He did note the many other slaves that stood watch or tended to the house as he followed Cervantes to where Rama was. The dominus' house was grander than anything he'd ever seen in his life. Concrete pillars, marble floors that shined. The many torches along his path illuminated the beautiful artwork that was painted on the walls in the form of murals, and Mateo found himself fascinated by such glamour.

"Keep pace," Cervantes chastised when he noticed Mateo drifting back.

"Apologies, doctore," Mateo said, then picked up his pace to keep up.

Mateo was led from the gladiator slave quarters, through the main house to the parlor where Rama laid on a divan as a female slave massaged his back. Cervantes presented him, then took several steps back, but not the armored guard, armed with a sword and dagger, who remained at Mateo's side.

Rama turned his head, looking at Mateo, his eyes scanning over his body with a certain scrutiny. "You've bulked up some. That is good. Your wound looks to be healing well."

Mateo nodded. "Yes, dominus."

"Good. I have sent message to the god, Eloy, of your virtue. I am expecting to hear back from him shortly. Have you even done anything with a man before?" Rama asked him.

Mateo's mouth was dry and he had to force himself to swallow in order to moisten his tongue so he could speak. "No, dominus."

"Even better." Rama moaned a little as the female slave's fingers kneaded a certain spot that rendered pleasure to their master. "You will be sent to the god, Eloy, and you will do whatever he demands of you without protest, without question, and without complaint, comprehend?"

The thought of being whored out to a god or anyone was detestable to Mateo, but he knew he had no choice. He wasn't looking forward to being a god's plaything, nor a gladiator. Still, he nodded because angering his dominus would only make his life harder than it already was.

"Yes, dominus."

"Good." Rama looked to Cervantes. "Make sure he is shaved in that area and under his arms."

Cervantes nodded. "Yes, dominus."

"You may go."

Cervantes stepped up, taking Mateo by his arm, and led him out of the room. Again, Mateo followed behind Cervantes as he was led back to his miserable cell. It wasn't until he was safely back behind bars did he dare ask Cervantes a question.

"Doctore, will it hurt?" he asked, wondering if being fucked in his ass was painful. He'd been teased by the other gladiators as they mocked him and his virginity. Many wondering how loud he'd scream once his cherry was popped.

Cervantes paused in his retreat and turned to Mateo. "It is said that the god, Eloy's, cock is a mighty member at twelve plentiful inches." He leaned against the bars, gripping them as he peered into Mateo's big, brown eyes. "He will rip you open, boy, and fuck you hard until he fills your insides with his seed. And you better be grateful for every second of it."

With that, Cervantes walked away, leaving Mateo with something new to fear.

Eloy had sent his response to Rama's offering by messenger the very next day, and eagerly anticipated the moment when the boy would arrive. Several hours had passed since he'd sent the reply and he was becoming a bit annoyed by how long it was taking for Mateo to come to him. Just when he felt his annoyance reaching a new peak, one of his servants knocked on his bedroom door.

"Enter," he called out.

The door opened and the servant stepped inside, dropping to one knee. "My god, Eloy. Your offering has arrived. Shall I send him inside?"

Eloy's lips curled up in a smile. "Yes."

The servant nodded and rose. He left the room and returned with Mateo at his side. Both men dropped to one knee, heads bowed.

"Leave us," Eloy ordered, and the servant obeyed. He stood up, and left, closing the door behind him. "Rise."

Mateo did as he was commanded, rising to his feet and keeping his gaze downcast.

Eloy stared at Mateo, thinking the boy was even more beautiful than he had been the last time he'd seen him. When he was on the sands, the boy had been weak and nearing emaciation, his skin had been covered in dirt and probably fecal matter. His hair had been matted and his body was bloody from his numerous wounds. But now, he could see everything the boy had to offer clearly, and he wanted it all.

Mateo was stunning with his big, brown eyes that held an innocence to them that was lost from many of the humans he was used to seeing. The shapely, full lips were something Eloy's gaze had focused on, as he couldn't help but imagine them wrapped around his cock, sucking his nectar from his balls. His eyes traveled down Mateo's body, drinking in his toned torso and strong, muscular limbs.

He could tell every curve and line was formed naturally, not molded like the other gladiators, probably because he'd not been trained yet. But the boy came from good stock. That was obvious. He liked how the boy had been bathed and oiled for his presentation. The scent of the oil was quite pleasing to Eloy's senses. There was a strong note of sandalwood, and it was a spice that could sing to his cock when he smelled it.

"Remove the loincloth," Eloy commanded. He watched the boy, with hands trembling, undo the knot of his loincloth. He didn't care that the boy was frightened or in awe, as most humans were. He only wanted what he wanted. He smiled as the piece of cloth fell to the marble floor, revealing Mateo's crotch. His cock was limp and looked to be four or five inches. Eloy wondered just how big it'd grow once the boy was aroused. It was time to find out.

Mateo stood before a god, naked and completely vulnerable. No matter how hard he tried, he couldn't still his trembling body. The whole trip there, he was terrified. What if the god was displeased with him and decided to kill him? The circumstances were different now than they were in the arena. What if the god felt like he'd made a mistake in sparing his life? Cervantes had done nothing to ease his anxiety on the way over, other than warn him of his punishment if he somehow angered the god.

Standing before him now, completely naked, Mateo couldn't take his eyes off Eloy as he remained silent. He'd never seen a being so beautiful that it literally took his breath away to behold him. He'd already been awestruck as he took in the sheer grandeur of the god's home. He'd even noticed the differences between this home and his dominus'. Where torches lined the walls to give light to the rooms and hallways, electrical lamps illuminated Eloy's home.

The furniture was different too; and the artwork, all of it handmade and painted. He'd heard of such luxuries in the stories told to him as a youth, but never had he ever imagined he'd see them. Even the bed the god laid in was a sight to see with its marble posts and thick mattress. A quick glance around the room showed even more opulence.

"Eyes on me!"

The snap in the command forced Mateo to turn back to Eloy.

"Apologies, God Eloy," Mateo said. He never thought he'd be in the presence of a god, and to make sure he didn't come off as rude, Cervantes had schooled him on how to address and behave in one's presence. He hoped he hadn't just messed up too much.

"Come closer," Eloy commanded.

Mateo obeyed, which brought him more into the light. Now that he was able to get a full view of the god, he could really see just how gorgeous Eloy was with his rippling muscles, dark hair, golden skin, and amber eyes. His jawline was strong and he smirked at him with a confidence no mortal man could muster. His eyes traveled between Eloy's legs as he wondered if what he'd heard was true. Was the god's cock really that big? He prayed that it wasn't.

"Come here," Eloy ordered.

Putting one foot in front of the other, Mateo moved forward, closer to Eloy until he was inches from him. The god slid to the edge of the bed, so he was now sitting upright. He reached up, running his hand over Mateo's chest. Mateo had never been touched like this. When the medicus touched him, it was to administer treatment. But this touch, it was so intimate and the look of desire in Eloy's amber eyes seem to burn, making the color of his eyes glow.

Eloy stroked his fingertips down the middle of Mateo's torso towards his cock, then he wrapped his fingers around Mateo's semi hard flesh.

"I see you enjoy my touch," Eloy said, then he looked up at Mateo. "So nervous. Have you ever known a man's touch? Surely, you've sucked cock before?"

Mateo swallowed hard as his body continued to tremble before the god. He shook his head. "No, God Eloy. You would be my first ever."

A wider smile spread across Eloy's lips as he relished his luck at having a true virgin in his grasp. He thought with how harsh the world was, Mateo would have had to have at least given a handjob or blowjob to someone, if not for food or clean water. The young man was full of surprises.

"Where are you from?" Eloy asked as he slowly started stroking Mateo's cock as his other hand began to play with Mateo's right nipple.

Mateo's chest heaved as he began to feel the most remarkable pleasure coursing through his body, all originating from what Eloy was doing to him.

"Th—the badlands, God Eloy," Mateo managed to say. He could feel his cheeks flushing with blood as the trembling of his body was replaced with sporadic quakes of pleasure.

Eloy snorted. "Ahh, I see. Which one?"

"The Kirrachi badlands of Airies, God Eloy," Mateo replied.

Eloy frowned. "I've never understood why people choose to live so far out. Explain it to me."

The conversation was hard for Mateo to focus on with everything else that was happening to him, but he tried his best. He balled his hands into fists, digging his nails into his palms to keep from getting lost in the ecstasy that he was experiencing. He looked down at Eloy and was met with the god's lusty but curious gaze. Also, he could tell that the god expected a truthful answer.

"I—I was born and raised there, God Eloy. You get used to it," he said.

"Why did your family stay?" Eloy asked as he rubbed his thumb over Mateo's sensitive cock.

"Ahhh, hunn," Mateo moaned and panted as his body quaked once more.

"Answer me," Eloy snapped.

"Please, God Eloy… it feels… it feels so good."

Eloy smirked. "I know. You are but a worthless human who is being pleasured by a god. I hope you can return my blessing with something remarkable both in my bed and in the arena." He pinched Mateo's nipple hard, causing him to cry out. "Answer my question. Tell me why you people live out there in that desolate land?" He hadn't bothered to find out before, but now having a badlander literally in his grasp, he wanted his curiosity quenched.

"Because corruption doesn't reach the badlands, God Eloy. My momma told me such. That's why we stay," Mateo said, then he whimpered as more pleasure coursed through him. He knew he wouldn't last too much longer. Especially not with the level of skill Eloy was manipulating him with.

"Corruption reaches everywhere, boy. Only now, it's what we manage. You humans can't seem to help yourselves in your greed and vanity," Eloy snarled.

"It is the greed and vanity of the gods we badlanders seek to avoid," Mateo said, and as soon as those words left his mouth, he wished he could have taken them back.

Eloy released Mateo's cock and nipple, then rose to his full height of six-foot-six. He towered over Mateo, so much so, the human had to look up at him.

He grabbed Mateo's jaw, squeezing it and making the human whine from the pain. "I should kill you for your insolence!"

"Apol—ow!" Mateo's attempt to make amends was thwart by more pain to his jaw as Eloy's powerful grip tightened.

"I spared your life in the arena for you to show me such disrespect!" Eloy roared. He released Mateo's jaw and quickly backhanded him, sending the human crashing to the floor and sliding a few feet from the force of the blow.

Mateo grunted, his body ached as he reached for the sore spot on his abdomen where he'd been stabbed. "Please, God Eloy… it is only what you asked of me. I told you why the people of the badlands stay," he pleaded as he grimaced in pain. The strike to his face shook his senses and left him a bit dizzy. His jaw ached and now, so did his cheek.

"The people of the badlands should be grateful that we have not sought out revenge for their blasphemy. Think that you or your parents' parents would have lived long enough to have birthed generations into the world if not for our benevolence?" Eloy roared in his rage as he stomped over to Mateo's prone figure.

Mateo held a hand up, surrendering. "No, my God Eloy. Please don't kill me."

Eloy stood over the human, his chest heaving in his anger. "It's arrogance like that, which is why we corrected this world. Healed it from human neglect. You live by our grace."

"Yes, God Eloy," Mateo said.

Eloy snarled and reached down, grabbing a handful of Mateo's dark, brown locks, and dragged him back over towards the bed. "I was going to show you mercy for your first time, but now I see badlanders don't recognize a god's mercy. So, I will give you what you expected."

With a harsh throw, Mateo was hauled up from the floor and tossed on the bed by his hair. The surface of his scalp throbbed with pain, but he wasn't allowed to recover from any of it as Eloy climbed on top of him, spreading his legs. Mateo was taken aback by how strong Eloy was. He had heard of the gods celestial powers surrounding the elements, but he was unaware of their physical abilities.

"Please!" Mateo begged. "Apologies, God Eloy. I only sought to please you, not to insult."

Eloy paused in his assault, he was already positioned between Mateo's legs. "Prove it."

Panting hard, Mateo managed to rise up a little, leaning on his elbows. "I am here to serve you, God Eloy, and to bring honor to the house of my dominus, Rama. I am grateful for your mercy to which you've shown my family, and me in the arena. Please forgive my foolishness, I humbly beg of you." He repeated the phrase Cervantes had taught him on the way over to use in case he'd misstepped as he had. It was the hope of Cervantes that the words would appease the god enough to forgive Mateo's blunders so the house of Rama would not be punished.

The words settled Eloy's rage and he leaned over the human, looking down at him. "That is how you seek forgiveness from a god, human. If you ever insult me or any of us in the future, your life will be forfeit."

Mateo nodded. "Yes, God Eloy." He released a sigh of relief that those words held resonance with the god and his life was once again spared.

Those baby browns of Mateo's eyes looking at him, pleading, heightened Eloy's desires. And those lips, oh those lips, how sweetly they trembled. Eloy felt his rage being replaced with lust once again and he leaned down, covering Mateo's mouth with his own. At first, the lips pressed against his were unyielding, uncertain, but then as he slipped his tongue between them, they began to soften and accept his kiss. Eloy felt his cock harden to the strength of steel between his legs and knew it was poking through his gold silk loincloth. He wanted this human!

Eloy used his restraint and pulled back from Mateo to look down at him. The young man's face was flushed, his cock rigid and pointing towards his navel, a sight that literally wet Eloy's tongue as he wanted to take Mateo's cock into his mouth. Something he rarely, oh so very rarely, did. The last human who he had pleasured with his mouth was eighty years ago. Loren was long since dead now and that was the last human who had sparked this amount of desire in him.

He wasn't sure if he was ready to give Mateo that much of him yet, regardless of how much his mouth wanted to feel the human's hot, hard flesh rubbing along his tongue as he licked and sucked on it. No, this was about him getting pleasure from an unsoiled male, not the other way around. He did like that Mateo was responding to him in such a positive manner. Perhaps the human was starting to understand how fortunate he was to be in his presence.

Mateo looked up at Eloy as the god removed his loincloth, revealing the huge cock that he'd heard so much about. His mouth dropped open in shock and the god smiled at his reaction.

"Oh yes, boy, you will take every inch of my cock. I will not stop until I've gained my satisfaction," Eloy smirked, then leaned over, snatching a bottle of oil from his nightstand. "Because you have proven that you appreciate the blessing I've given you, I'll show you this one mercy."

"Gr—gr—gratitude, g—God Eloy," Mateo stuttered. His fear was returning in spades, seeing the god pour oil on the length of his huge cock. He'd never had anything go inside of his asshole before. Let alone something the size of the large cucumber he saw in the market the day he had arrived at the slave auction.

Frightened, he began to tense, his muscles constricting as if they could protect him from what was coming. Eloy looked down at him and shook his head.

"You only make it worse by tensing, boy. You should be grateful to take a god inside of your body. Is this you rejecting me?" Eloy asked, one eyebrow cocked.

Panic set in and Mateo shouted, "No!" His eyes bulged when he saw the frown appear on Eloy's face. "Apologies, God Eloy. No, I fear the pain, it's my first," he said, hoping to correct his offense. He noticed the gods, at least this one in particular, seemed to take words as insult very easily. Something he wasn't used to, and he didn't want to suffer the god's wrath or Rama's.

Eloy pressed the tip of his cock against Mateo's virgin hole. "Even the pain I'll give you is a blessing, boy," he said, then he pushed forward, entering without hesitation.

"Ahhhh!" Mateo screamed, his back arching as he braced against the agony of the huge cock forcing itself inside of him. He gripped the sheets as Eloy pushed deeper, the pain so intense, his screams were cut off. He closed his eyes tightly and gritted his teeth together as he groaned. Tears breached his eyes and rolled down the sides of his face as he endured yet another bout of pain at the hands of those who'd called themselves his superiors.

"Take it!" Eloy growled as he pulled back and pushed inside Mateo again and again, milking his cock inside the human's asshole.

The pleasure he felt was amazing as he relished the tight heat Mateo's body offered. "Oooh, nothing is more perfect for a god's cock than a virgin's cunt." He was lost in ecstasy as he fucked Mateo, each thrust sending him deeper into that vortex of sexual bliss.

Mateo, unfortunately, was having a totally different experience. He was stretched to his limits as Eloy's cock continued to ram him. His asshole burned with every drag of the god's cock along his anal passage. He didn't feel blessed, or even lucky, to have been the one to receive Eloy's favor at the moment. All he felt was pain, and all he wanted was for it to end. The god stared down at him, his amber gaze burning with a fiery glow as he continued to fuck him. Mateo could actually see the red and yellow embers flickering in Eloy's irises. The sight was majestic, beautiful and terrifying all at the same time.

Eloy seemed lost in the moment, completely oblivious to the pain he was causing, at least that was how Mateo saw it. He couldn't connect with Eloy mentally, even as they were connected physically. Mateo was painfully aware of the time, and it seemed to drag on with every second the god rocked against him.

Finally, the moment came that he'd been hoping for. Eloy's body stiffened, Mateo could see his veins and muscles protruding beneath his flesh, and knew the god was about to reach his climax. At least it was about to be over. Two more pumps and it happened. Eloy threw his head back, roaring loudly and grunting as his body released. Mateo could feel the hot seed squirting inside of him, splashing against his anal walls, and it seemed like an endless flow. He could even feel it dribbling out of his hole as Eloy pumped more into him. Finally, Eloy's body quaked a few more times before he pulled his cock free of Mateo's body.

Oh, thank god, it's over, Mateo thought as he released a long sigh.

Eloy looked down, satisfied to see his flesh wet and slick with various fluids, some of it blood. A sure sign that he'd fully claimed Mateo's virginity. He leaned over the human, who was laying on his bed and looking up at him with the same uncertainty that had been on his face when he'd first entered his bedroom.

"My cock and seed has claimed your chastity. You may go," Eloy said, dismissing Mateo.

Mateo sat up and began scooting off the bed, which had been the only thing he had enjoyed for its soft comfort during the rough treatment. The whole experience was empty and left him feeling less than human. What little worth he seemed to have before it happened was now gone. He limped towards his discarded loincloth, picking it up and tying it around his waist. The thin fabric concealed his ass and cock, which was better than being naked at the moment. As he was heading for the door, Eloy called out to him, which prompted him to turn and face the cruel god.

"Yes, God Eloy?" he asked.

"What do you say for the blessing I've given you?" Eloy asked as he lounged on his bed, legs spread wide so Mateo could get a good look at the cock that had just ripped away what little innocence he had.

"Gratitude, God Eloy," Mateo said, knowing that was what the god wanted to hear.

Eloy nodded, and Mateo left the room. A human servant walked up to him. "Your doctore awaits," the servant said, and led Mateo through the luxurious home with its marble pillars and floors, glass chandeliers, hand-carved wood frames and crowning, and beautifully wallpapered walls. Such finery wasted on gods who took it all for granted, as far as he was concerned.

Cervantes waited beside the carriage and opened the door for him to climb inside and he did, taking a seat—gingerly so. Cervantes climbed in after him and motioned for the driver to leave. The two horses reared into action and began trotting down the road back to their ludus.

"You're a man now, Mateo," Cervantes said as he stared at the slave. "A boy walked inside that home and a man came out."

Mateo looked at Cervantes. "Why am I a man, doctore?"

"Virginity is for children and young girls. Not men destined for greatness inside the arena. Doesn't matter if you enjoyed it or not, it is done. A rite of passage that really should have been traveled before now. You're nineteen, most males have it taken at fifteen or sixteen."

"So young," Mateo whispered in retrospection.

Cervantes snorted. "Young? Hardly. A boy's cunt can be stretched to fit a cock. And when it's done, they too are men. You should appreciate the pain you're feeling. A god gave it to you, a rarity to lose ones virginity to a divine being."

Mateo didn't want to feel grateful for what had happened to him in Eloy's bedroom, no more than he wanted to feel grateful for being kidnapped from his homelands and sold into slavery. He adjusted himself on the wood bench inside the carriage, which was unforgiving. The pain in his asshole throbbed and he shifted to one ass cheek to try to alleviate the agony.

Cervantes smirked, then leaned forward, thrusting his hand between Mateo's legs. Instinctually, Mateo grabbed Cervantes' wrist, stopping him from going further.

Cervantes expression hardened, his lips turning up in a sneer. "Remove your hand, now," he growled.

Mateo released Cervantes' wrist, even though he didn't want to.

"Don't ever do that again, filth. You may have been spared by a god, but you are still a fucking slave!" Cervantes reminded. "You will endure whatever your dominus and doctore put on you. I would give you lashes for this offense if you weren't already healing from injuries. Next time you seek to stop me or anyone else above your status, I will. Comprehend?"

Once again, Mateo had to face the ugly reality that he was nothing in the eyes of those around him and he nodded. "Yes, doctore."

"Good." Cervantes, now with his wrist freed, thrust his hand further between Mateo's legs. "Open them!"

Mateo widened his legs, giving himself to yet another male this night. He felt Cervantes fingers probing his battered hole, one of the man's fat digits wiggled its way inside, past his sphincter, and he grimaced in pain.

"Ahh, yes… the god, Eloy, had his way with you. I told you he would. You're swollen, but you'll heal. Mmmm, still wet with his seed. Works fine for me," Cervantes said, pulling his finger out of

Mateo's ass. He looked at his blood and cum covered finger and smiled. "The sign of a good fuck."

Mateo didn't say anything as he looked at Cervantes examining his finger.

"We have a while before we get home. I'll taste what the god, Eloy, has had now," Cervantes said as he began unbuckling his belt and undoing the buttons of his leather pants. He pulled out his dirty, fat cock. It had some girth to it, but not nearly as big as Eloy's. Still, it wasn't anything Mateo wanted inside of him.

"Please, doctore, it hurts," Mateo pleaded.

Cervantes slapped him hard across his cheek, the same one Eloy had bruised. He fell to the side, hitting his head on the wood door. The pain shot across his noggin, sending sparks into his vision a second before it cleared up. He turned, looking at Cervantes.

"Be a man! Don't cry to me about pain. You don't know what pain is. You'll endure this and ten times this if you're lucky to live so long. Now, get over here and ride my cock," the doctore commanded. "You should get used to having a man inside your cunt. As pretty as you are, you'll experience it quite often from Rama and the other gladiators. At least until you rise in status as one of them."

If that wasn't motivation enough, Mateo didn't know what was. He was now even more determined to succeed in his gladiator training so he could no longer be used. The protection that he had before was now gone since he was not a virgin. Now, gladiators like Boris would have free reign over him. The thought terrified as much as it repulsed.

Agitated by how long it was taking Mateo to obey his command, Cervantes reached over, grabbing hold of Mateo's balls, and squeezed.

"Arghhh!" Mateo growled out through gritted teeth and tightly clenched eyes.

"These balls are boy balls still, I see. Don't worry. I will toughen them up or cut them off. You'll either be a man or a eunuch, which is a male not worthy of his manhood. Choose now which you will be." Cervantes gave Mateo's nutsac one good tug, then released it. He settled back onto his bench and waited to see if Mateo would climb onto his cock or still sit there and whine.

Mateo cradled his balls tenderly, but knew he didn't have the option to not obey. He was risking his opportunity to rise by refusing to fuck Cervantes and maybe everyone else at the Ludus, until he was a gladiator on equal standing with the others. But even then, he'd still be a slave and would have to follow his dominus' command at any time.

Making the hard decision to ignore his own misery, he released his aching ball sac and climbed over to Cervantes, taking his place on his lap.

"You can learn. That is good. Now, make me hard," Cervantes ordered.

The command left Mateo somewhat confused as he didn't know exactly what Cervantes meant. "What would you have me do, doctore?"

Cervantes rolled his eyes. "Did you not do anything in the badlands? Not even to your own cock, boy?"

Ahh, it dawned on him what Cervantes was asking. Mateo nodded and reached down between them, grasping the doctore's fat, stubby cock and began stroking. It was his first time touching a cock that wasn't his own, but even as he worked his hand up and down the man's shaft, he knew it wouldn't be his last. He watched and listened as Cervantes moaned while his cock grew harder and longer. The foreskin pulled back with each stroke, revealing smega and sweat that had a stench that was offensive to Mateo. Cervantes didn't seem to care about his unclean flesh and only wanted pleasure.

The man looked to be about five inches fully erect, and not as wide as Eloy had been, so maybe that was a blessing Mateo could take into account. He knew what he had to do next and he raised up, only to slide down on Cervantes unwashed cock. Once again, he felt the pain of being stretched and still being sensitive from his brutal first time, this second try didn't seem like it was going to be better.

Mateo sat down, completely burying Cervantes inside him, to the other man's delight. He began to rise again and sit back down, and Cervantes moaned in satisfaction as his cock was incased in the tight, hot, and wet cavern of Mateo's ass. He didn't care that it hurt the boy, only that he got enjoyment.

"Aye, ride my cock, boy. Show me what a man you are," Cervantes said, grinning with a mixture of insensitivity and lust.

Mateo held onto Cervantes' shoulders and balanced himself on the man's lap as he bounced up and down on his cock. The rocking of the carriage itself helped as much as it hindered, making it harder for Mateo to sit in one place, but easier to rock back and forth.

"Oh…oh…oh yes… oh that's it. Oh, what a sweet cunt," Cervantes panted as the pleasure took him. He wrapped his arms around Mateo's back, holding him in place as they fucked. The boy felt so good to him, he could feel his orgasm approaching. He would indeed have his way with Mateo again one day soon. Especially since his dominus had already given him permission. Mateo would be free to fuck as soon as the god, Eloy, was done with him, that had been the command. Three weeks had been a long time coming as far as Cervantes was concerned.

Mateo continued to ride Cervantes, hating every second of the man's bad breath blowing in his face with each of his lust-filled pants. He'd heard stories of how pleasurable sex could be, certainly Eloy and Cervantes were enjoying it. He wondered if sex was ever pleasurable for both involved or just the one whose cock was being stroked.

His asshole continued to burn as he fucked Cervantes, but he made sure to bounce as he rocked, which seemed to please Cervantes. He was relieved when the moment came when the doctore's cock stiffened inside of him. Once again, he felt a male's cock shoot its seed inside of him. Cervantes huffed and groaned as he shook during his orgasm. It looked like something Mateo might want to feel, but he wasn't sure if he ever would.

Afterward, he climbed off Cervantes' lap, the man's cock thankfully free of his asshole. He sat back down on the bench and tried very hard not to show how much discomfort he was feeling, as that only seemed to upset Cervantes.

"That was good," Cervantes said after a few minutes had passed between them. His cock was now tucked safely back into his pants, his belt buckled. "If you'd been sold to a brothel, they'd teach you how to work your hips more. Your mouth would be another amazing feature to pleasure man or woman." Cervantes leaned over, grabbing Mateo's chin. "Mmmm, and you have such a pretty mouth."

Please don't ask me to suck it, Mateo prayed silently.

Cervantes released Mateo's chin and settled back into his seat. "So, how did it feel to have a god inside of you?"

Mateo looked at Cervantes. He had to think hard about his reply and quickly. These were people who worshipped the gods, and any negativity might get him punished. If he was going to survive this new life, he was going to have to learn how to play the game.

"A pleasure and honor to have my first time to be with him, doctore," Mateo lied.

Cervantes smiled and nodded. "You learn."

That comment left Mateo a little bit confused. Did Cervantes really know the truth behind his words? Maybe he did, it wasn't as if he had held his emotions well behind a mask when he first saw him after having sex with Eloy. But perhaps the doctore was praising him for not speaking his mind. Yes, he was learning.

CHAPTER NINE

An hour later, they were back at the ludus. Cervantes climbed out of the carriage first, then Mateo, who moved a bit slower. He followed Cervantes to where the medicus, Tomas, tended to patients, and motioned for a guard to fetch the physician. While they waited, he watched over Mateo, who was now leaning slightly on the gurney.

The medicus entered. "Is he badly torn?" he asked, walking over toward Mateo.

"There are tears and he is swollen. The god, Eloy, used him properly," Cervantes stated.

"Lean over, boy," the medicus said.

Mateo did as he was told, leaning over even more while the medicus inspected his asshole.

"Ahh, very swollen indeed," the medicus said.

"He's taken two cocks tonight, and will take more," Cervantes stated.

"Aye, but tonight he should rest, and the next day. Remember, you want him strong and ready to train. His wounds still require healing and now this," the medicus pointed to Mateo's ass.

Cervantes huffed. "He's young, strong, he will begin his training tomorrow—light," he added once he saw the disapproving frown on the medicus' face. "Light training. Dominus' orders."

Tomas sighed. "Very well. Still tonight, he rests."

"Give him the salve and release him into my care," Cervantes commanded.

Mateo really didn't know if Cervantes outranked Tomas or if they were on equal standing. Both slaves, but with prestigious positions of power among the rest. He'd only been there three weeks and still, he had so many questions.

"I'll clean him first, then salve him," the medicus said.

"Make haste," Cervantes snapped.

Mateo kept quiet as the medicus flushed his insides out of the cum and blood. The solution stung, but also offered some measure of reprieve from the pain. The salve that was added after really gave him comfort and the cooling sensation gave him the relief he'd been dying for. Now that that was done, he walked back to his cell with Cervantes, who locked him back inside.

"Tomorrow, we begin your training. Also, this is your last night in this cell. Take that as you will," Cervantes said, then walked away.

Mateo slunk down to the floor, his body aching, his feelings hurting and spirit nearly broken. But he still had hope that one day, he would be free.

Something hard nudged Mateo in his side repeatedly, which yanked him out of his blissful sleep. He opened his eyes and looked up to see Kodac looking down at him.

"Rise, we train," the big, black gladiator-guard said.

As much as Mateo wanted to just close his eyes and return to the dreamland he'd been in, he knew he didn't have a choice. He rose to his feet, wincing a little from the pain in his ass and side from his still-healing wounds. He followed behind Kodac as he led him out into the courtyard where the other gladiators were already assembled and preparing to practice.

Kodac led him over to a table which had several articles of training gear on it. He picked up a rawhide vest and began placing it on Mateo's torso. He tied the sides together, securing the vest.

"Hold out hands," Kodac said.

Mateo obeyed, holding up both of his hands while Kodac began wrapping his palms and wrists in strips of leather, binding them. Next, he picked up a wooden katana and a wakizashi, handing them both to Mateo.

"You will train in the style of Sakata, a fine gladiator. The first to use this style. Go to Cervantes," Kodac ordered.

Mateo examined the two swords he held in his hands, they each had their own heft to them; the katana felt like it was at least two pounds and the wakizashi felt like it was over a pound. He'd never seen two swords that looked like them, but he liked their design. Following the order given, he made his way towards Cervantes, but he also checked out the other gladiators as they began to train.

Boris was working with a long sword that looked to be as tall as he was. Shian, the would-be pretty gladiator, had not half his face been scarred and he still had both eyes, was working with another weapon new to Mateo. But if he had to put a name to it, it looked like a whip sword, and the other gladiators steered clear of the more petite one as he worked the whip-like blades with intricate precision.

"Our dominus has the best gladiators, you will be no exception," Cervantes said. His voice bringing Mateo's attention to him.

"Yes, doctore, I do want to fight good," Mateo said.

"Not good, best," Cervantes corrected. He then began to instruct him on how he should hold his swords. He also informed him that he could wear them sheathed at his side and use one sword or both during a fight and that he'd be trained in both styles, as was the style of Sakata.

"Why are there different fighting styles, doctore?" Mateo asked.

"Each man or woman is different. They need to fight differently. You would not fight well with Boris' broad sword, as Boris would not fight well with Feilong's twin jamadhars," Cervantes said.

Mateo turned to look at the mentioned gladiators again, now knowing what their weapons were called. He looked at Feilong stabbing at a block of wood with two daggers that looked like long scissors and blades at the same time. It was a deadly weapon that he was happy to not have been stabbed by. He doubted he would have survived.

He couldn't help it, his gaze landed on Haraka as he watched him spar with another gladiator whose name he didn't know. Both worked with wooden swords and shields and Mateo did have to acknowledge the skill with which both men wielded their weapons. If Haraka wasn't a champion, he knew his own skill would have to surpass the man who'd nearly brought him to death.

"Pay attention," Cervantes said, then punctuated the command by slapping Mateo in his injured side with his blade.

"Ah!" Mateo gasped, and then groaned as his side throbbed. Luckily, the rawhide vest took the blunt of the blow. "Apologies, doctore."

After that blunder, he made sure to keep his attention on his trainer. For hours, he practiced stances using both swords. Defensive and offensive. Then he had lunch, which was oatmeal, wheat bread, and water. It was better than the broth, but he really wanted the beef stew and rolls the gladiators feasted on. Once they had all eaten, it was back to training. Some sparred with each other, some spared alone, and others did the physical exercises needed to keep their bodies in shape. Mateo had to join them, although his exercises were limited.

The dominus wanted him to start his training, but not to reinjure himself, which was why he'd been treated with a certain level of delicacy, which Mateo appreciated. Although, he wasn't too naive to believe that it would always be like that. If last night was any proof, the kid gloves were slowly coming off.

The ache in his body was annoying, but not too distracting as he worked up another load of sweat, conditioning his body to be able to survive the world he was now a part of. Throughout his training, he knew he'd caught the attention of a few of the gladiators. He could hear their gossip, some thinking he'd never survive to become a gladiator and others only wanted to fuck him. As it was, he was the youngest there and as luck would have it, the most handsome. Two attributes Rama and Cervantes had already taken advantage of.

At the end of their day, Mateo practically had to drag himself back to his cell, but when he tried to enter, Kodac stopped him. He turned, facing the menacing gladiator-guard.

"What is wrong?" he asked.

"You will bathe first, wash the stink of the day off your body, then you will see dominus. Put the oil on your body after you bathe, our dominus likes that," Kodac informed him.

The words weighed heavily on Mateo. Twenty-four hours ago, he was untouched, and now it seemed like everyone wanted to touch him, and in ways he didn't desire. His body was full of exhaustion and merciless pain, and yet, he knew his dominus would want to fuck his already sore asshole. He only hoped that afterward, he would be able to sleep peacefully.

Following the command, he made his way to the communal bath where all of the gladiators were gathered and washing the filth of the day off in the warm waters of three huge, deep bathtubs. Removing his loincloth, he climbed inside one of the tubs with the least men inside of it. He could feel eyes on him and hoped they'd only look and nothing more. To his disappointment, Boris climbed out of the tub he was in and into the one Mateo was now bathing in.

"You not so protected by bars now," Boris said as he saddled up close to Mateo, pressing his hairy chest to Mateo's arm.

In the earlier days since arriving at the ludus, Mateo had been meek, afraid and uncertain of what would be his fate. He now had some understanding, and he also began to see that if he were to survive, he had to cast away whatever timid feelings he had. He was in a world of warriors and barbarians. They were used to taking what they wanted, giving no apologies, and killing for sport and glory. If he was going to rise in status, he had to become someone new, someone without fear and doubt. He had to become a gladiator.

He turned to Boris. "Leave me be."

Boris grinned, his hand shooting out, grasping Mateo's chin, pushing his head back. "The little bird squawks at the condor."

"Even a bird of prey is prey to something else," Mateo said.

Boris growled and pressed himself up harder to Mateo, pinning him against the edge of the tub. The water splashed between the two as they faced off.

"Grab my cock," Boris ordered.

Mateo could feel the man's hardness pressed against his stomach, as Boris was much taller than he was. The man's bad breath pelted his face, but he refused to acknowledge it. He was sure his own breath didn't smell all too pleasant either, not that it seemed to matter to Boris.

"No," Mateo protested.

"Fine," Boris said, then he released Mateo's chin and grabbed his shoulders, trying to force him to turn around. None of the other gladiators stepped in to help, and Mateo knew they all wanted to see if he'd fight or be taken. And even if he was still taken, would it be without a fight? Mateo knew this was a moment where he had to make a stand or he'd end up being their whore, which was something he didn't want.

"No!" Mateo yelled as he pushed back against Boris' powerfully toned and hairy chest. The hair was what caught Mateo's eye and he gripped a thick patch of it and yanked as hard as he could.

"Argh! Bitch!" Boris yelled in pain as several strands of his chest hair came out in Mateo's fist. The other gladiators laughed at the attack, thinking it a smart one.

"Looks like the lamb is turning into a wolf," one of the men said as he approached the two. He'd already been bathing in the tub and he stepped up to both men. Mateo looked at him and then at Boris, feeling like they were about to gang up on him. The man put his arm around Mateo's shoulders, pulling him closer. "Did you like that cock in your cunt, boy?"

"I'm not a boy," Mateo snapped.

More chuckles from the crowd ensued. Some of the men returned to their bathing, while others began to take part in each other, groping bodies and sucking flesh.

"Look at them," the gladiator said, pointing to three men in the corner of the tub across from theirs. Mateo turned to see the men caressing each other and fondling each other's cocks as they kissed. The sight did entice Mateo, especially now that he had some idea of what a man's body pressed against his felt like. Before Eloy had savagely taken him, he was aroused by how nice it felt to have the god between his legs.

"I don't wish to do that with you," Mateo said, putting his foot down. Not only was he expected to fuck their dominus after his bath, but he didn't desire these two men. He didn't desire any of them at the moment.

"I don't care what you wish," Boris snapped and pressed his body back against Mateo's.

"His asshole is probably raw after being fucked by a god," Feilong said as he rubbed oil on his body. "Give him a few days before you plunder him."

"Mind your cunt business, Feilong," Boris retorted. He began to rub his cock along Mateo's stomach. "Yeah, that feels good."

The other gladiator grabbed Mateo's chin, bringing his face to his. "You should play with us," he said before forcing Mateo to kiss him. "Ah!" he yelled and pulled back, his lip bleeding from the wound Mateo had given him.

More laughter from the others as they looked on.

"He's more than you can handle, you two?" Hans asked.

"I'll have his cunt!" Boris growled, then he grabbed Mateo by the back of his thighs, hoisting him up. Mateo brought his arm up and elbowed Boris in his nose, breaking the bone. Boris grunted in pain and released him as he stumbled back in the water. More laughter broke out as they watched the big gladiator cradle his bleeding nose.

"Enough!" Cervantes' deep tenor rang out, silencing the laughter and chatter. Even the men who were fucking stopped and turned to their doctore. "Boris, Gregor… his cunt won't be yours tonight. Boris, come here."

The hulking gladiator gave a long, evil glare at Mateo as he climbed out of the tub. Then he turned and walked over to Cervantes, who began to examine his nose. Boris groaned a little as the doctore pressed on his bridge a little.

"It's broken," Cervantes confirmed. He turned to Mateo. "You did this?"

Mateo nodded. "Yes, doctore." He wasn't sure if he'd just earned himself a punishment or not, but he'd take it.

Cervantes snorted, then looked back at Boris. "Wet your cock with another's cunt tonight. First, go to the medicus to get that set."

"Yes, doctore," Boris said, then walked past Cervantes as he left the bathing area.

Cervantes looked at the others. "Bathe, fuck, gossip as you bitches like to do. Tomorrow, I will train the shit out of you lot."

There were some chuckles at that statement from some of the men. Others continued to have sex as if they'd never been interrupted.

Cervantes looked at Mateo. "You, finish and oil up. Now."

"Yes, doctore," Mateo said, then he quickly finished bathing. Gregor had backed up to let him, but he kept his eyes on Mateo the entire time as he stroked his cock. Mateo made sure to keep tossing warning glances the gladiator's way, hoping to keep him at bay. He climbed out of the tub and walked over to the bottle of oil Feilong had been using and began to pour the contents into the palm of his hand. Next, he rubbed the sandalwood-scented oil over his entire body. He liked how soft and smooth his skin felt with the oil on it, as he had the night before. Before leaving the bathing area to join Cervantes, who had been watching over the men as Mateo prepared himself, he grabbed his loincloth off the floor.

"Come," Cervantes said, and Mateo followed. "You did good breaking Boris' nose. Leave the boy behind and be a man."

"Yes, doctore," Mateo replied. He, of course, was terrified when he'd broken the gladiator's nose, but he made sure that fear never surfaced. The other gladiators would have only looked down on him if it had. He wasn't sure if he'd be able to fight Boris or Gregor off if they went for him again, but he'd try.

Mateo was led through the dominus' home, and after leaving Eloy's palace, his dominus's home didn't look as luxurious as it had before. However, it was still something that Mateo marveled over.

"Doctore, why does the dominus use candles and torches instead of lamps like the god, Eloy, does?" Mateo asked.

Cervantes stopped and turned to him. "Keep that question to yourself in the future," he growled, then continued to lead him to Rama's bedroom.

It seemed like an innocent enough question, but Mateo didn't bother to press. "Apologies, doctore."

Cervantes didn't respond. They stopped outside of an oak door and he turned to face Mateo. "You belong to dominus, remember that."

Mateo nodded, understanding the meaning behind the words. "Yes, doctore."

Cervantes knocked on the door, and when Rama called out, he opened it and stepped aside. "The whelp, dominus," he said, then motioned for Mateo to enter.

Mateo didn't much like the names he'd been called since being kidnapped, but he knew better than to mouth off about it or to even show it bothered him. Doing so would only get him more disrespect. He walked into the bedroom and stood at attention to await further commands.

"Leave us," Rama said as he gazed at Mateo.

Cervantes obeyed, closing the door behind him.

"Come here, boy," Rama said, and patted the side of his bed.

Mateo walked over to the bed and sat down.

"Closer," Rama commanded.

Mateo scooted closer. Dissatisfied with the closeness, Rama reached out, grabbing Mateo's shoulder, and yanked him back until he was laying on the bed. Then he wrapped his arms around Mateo, pulling him closer to his body.

"There, that's better," Rama stated, grinning as he looked down the length of Mateo's body. He rubbed his hand over Mateo's chest, his fingers playing with Mateo's nipples. "How did it feel to have the god, Eloy, pump his cock and seed into you?"

It was a question that everyone seemed to want an answer to. But the answer they wanted was a lie, so Mateo told it. "It was very pleasurable, dominus. I can still feel him inside me." That last part was true. He could still feel Eloy's cock inside of him, and the phantom sensation haunted him. The heat of the god's seed was seared into his memories as much as the pain of his entry was.

Rama growled low, his lust evident in the tone and in his eyes. "Oooh, to place my cock where a god's has been is always an honor." He ripped the loincloth from Mateo's waist, revealing his cock and balls. "Did he touch you here?" he asked as he fondled Mateo's shaft.

Mateo forced himself not to cringe away from the touch of his dominus, repulsive as it was. The man's massive belly pressed harder to his side as Rama began to rub himself against Mateo.

"He did, dominus," Mateo replied. He remembered how good it felt to have Eloy touch him in his most private area. Or how fantastic it felt to have his nipples played with. Rama was messing with his nipples now, but the effect wasn't the same. Where Eloy's touch had made blood rush to harden his cock, Rama's touch was the opposite.

Again, Rama growled in lust, then leaned over, taking Mateo's nipple into his mouth. He sucked and nipped the little nub of flesh and fantasized over how much Eloy enjoyed doing the same, as Mateo had such delectable nipples. He continued to stroke Mateo's cock and after a few minutes, he stopped sucking the boy's nipples and looked at him.

"Why is your cock not hard?" he asked.

Mateo cocked both eyebrows, surprised by the question, which he didn't have a true answer that wouldn't offend. So, he made up one that would suffice. "My body is exhausted, dominus. So much training and sore still. Apologies for not being able to perform for you." The truth was, Rama disgusted him and he found his touch to be nauseating.

Rama frowned, his eyebrow crinkling deeply. "Apologies, indeed." He released Mateo's flaccid cock and sat up. "Is your cunt exhausted too?"

Actually, it was, but he knew that was also something his dominus didn't want to hear. "No, dominus," he lied.

"It better not be," Rama said as he positioned himself between Mateo's legs. "Did you oil your cunt?"

As a matter of fact, he had because the oil was so soothing there. He nodded. "Yes, dominus."

Without saying another word, Rama positioned his dick at Mateo's hole, then pushed. Mateo gripped the sheets and gasped in pain as once again, he was being brutally breached. His only comfort was that Rama wasn't nearly as long or wide as Eloy had been, or even Cervantes. He spread his legs wider to allow Rama to pump his hips without his gut getting in the way.

Of course, physically, Rama was out of Eloy's range, but that wasn't why Mateo was repulsed by the man. This was the same man who'd offered him piss instead of water when he'd been so thirsty the first night here. Shit for food if he pressed the matter. The same man who'd thought nothing of his life and sent him into an arena to die, on top of being weak and starved. The only bit of kindness, if it could be called that, Rama had given him was solely for his own purposes as he'd given him to a god to use as Eloy saw fit. No, Rama wasn't a man Mateo could feel desire for.

He laid still, forcing himself to stay relaxed as Rama rocked back and forth on top of him, thrusting his cock in and out of his ass as he huffed and puffed in labored breaths. Mateo wondered why men seemed to enjoy doing this so much, for he didn't see the appeal. He'd watched, night after night, the other gladiators having sex, and the man getting a cock in his ass seemed to really like the feeling. He wondered why he'd been cheated, or were they faking it?

Rama's hips stuttered and his body stiffened. To Mateo's delight, it didn't take long for his dominus to reach his climax. Several grunts later, Rama emptied his balls inside Mateo, then pulled out, collapsing on his back next to him.

"So tight... such a... tight cunt," Rama panted.

Mateo didn't say anything, as he wasn't really being spoken to. He only hoped he could be dismissed now that Rama had gotten his satisfaction. A few more minutes passed, and then he got his wish. Rama called out to Cervantes, who opened the door.

"Take him back," Rama said.

Cervantes nodded. "Yes, dominus."

Mateo quickly climbed out of the bed, grabbing his loincloth with him, which he wrapped around his waist as he made his way out of the bedroom. Cervantes walked behind him this time and he could feel the doctore's eyes on his back.

"Doctore?" Mateo asked after his curiosity got the better of him.

"Your cock was soft and dry, why?"

Well, that was a question he wasn't expecting. "I'm still sore, doctore."

"So?" Cervantes grabbed Mateo's arm, whirling him around and slamming him against the wall. He reached under Mateo's loincloth, grabbing his cock and began stroking. "Get hard."

"I—I don't know if I can, doctore," Mateo said.

"This is survival, boy! Do you think our dominus was pleased with your limp dick?"

That was something Mateo hadn't thought about. "No, doctore?"

"Get hard, now," Cervantes ordered.

Like Rama, Cervantes wasn't a man that appealed to Mateo. He remembered it was his cock that he'd had to drink piss from and his cruelty that gave him no regard until now. Did Cervantes really want to teach him something or was he just exerting more of his dominance over him? Either way, one thing rang true, this was survival. Mateo closed his eyes and thought about something that did speak to his body in ways he wasn't used to.

Eloy.

Eloy's amber eyes boring into his. Eloy's powerful god body pressed against his. Eloy's hands manipulating his flesh the way he wanted and Eloy's voice in his ear. So much promise that night could have held had he not angered the god, or perhaps, had the god not been so easily angered. He began to feel tingles flowing through him, radiating from his cock, and he moaned.

"Ahhh, good. What are you thinking about?" Cervantes asked as he continued to stroke Mateo.

Mateo moaned as pleasure began to ripple through him. "Eloy, doctore," he said without thinking, even forgetting to give Eloy his title.

"I see," Cervantes said as he continued to work Mateo's cock, making sure to rub his thumb over the young gladiator-in-training's head, smearing his precum over the tip. "Yeah, get it wet. Feels good now?"

Mateo nodded and made sure to keep his eyes closed so as not to lose his fantasy. "Yes, doctore." His breathing began to intensify as he felt his orgasm growing. The last time he had one had been before he'd been taken, and only by his own hand. This was the first time another person had given him one.

"You're a man now. Cum like one, and remember what brought you to the end," Cervantes said.

Mateo nodded as his chest heaved. He moaned and gripped Cervantes' shoulders. "Ahh, ahhh fuck," he gasped.

"Yeah, that's it... don't hold back. Cum," Cervantes encouraged.

Mateo's breath was coming harder now as Cervantes' strokes quickened their pace. His balls started tingling as they drew up, ready to release their load. "Uh, unn, I'm cumming," he said, almost surprised by the outcome.

Cervantes grinned as he watched the young man's body quake and felt his hot release cascading down his fingers as he continued to milk Mateo through his climax. He'd done this very same thing with every gladiator who had entered those walls and for various reasons. Some men, in spite of the fact, fought better having shot off a load before hitting the sands.

He'd take them aside and jerked them off before it was their time. Others, it was to cure their anxiety. Some, only because he wanted them to cum in his hand and see the look of pleasure on their faces as they gave into him. For Mateo, it was to teach him how to survive. He knew the man wasn't attracted to him or their dominus. But if he ever failed to perform for their dominus again, it could result in him having to beat Mateo for displeasing Rama. Something he'd do if he had to, but it would only set him back in his training as he healed. The other reason was because he wanted to see Mateo's beautiful face in the throes of sexual release.

"Feel better?" Cervantes asked Mateo as he wiped his hand clean of Mateo's cum on his loincloth.

Mateo opened his eyes and nodded. "Yes, doctore."

"Whatever got you through that, you hold on to the next time our dominus sticks his cock inside your cunt or you may be punished for being so insulting," Cervantes warned, and Mateo straightened his back.

"Yes, doctore," Mateo said, realizing why this little transaction had happened.

"You won't always be exhausted when he calls on you." With that, Cervantes motioned for Mateo to keep walking, and he did, all the way past the cell he had been sleeping in to the gladiator barracks where the men were lounging or sleeping.

"I'm not to sleep in the cell anymore, doctore?" Mateo asked.

Cervantes shook his head. "You may not have earned the mark of a gladiator, but you will bunk with them. If you survive your test, these will be your brothers upon the sand."

Mateo turned back to the men and began making his way to an empty cot in the corner of the room. He laid down, pulling the sheet over his body. He could still feel Rama's seed inside his asshole, but the pleasure of his orgasm made him relaxed enough not to care. Cervantes took one more look around, then left the men to their slumber. And sleep, Mateo did.

CHAPTER TEN

Three more weeks into training, Mateo was getting used to handling two swords. Cervantes took no mercy on him as they trained, but at least his wound was practically healed. The gladiators had given him some respect as they'd been witness to his training and the dedication he'd put into it. He'd been alternating between steel and wood so that he was used to both as he practiced parrying attacks and other defensive and offensive maneuvers.

Feilong had once told him the origins of the style in which he trained, saying it was a form of kenjutsu from Japan. Of course, the country of Japan had long since been destroyed in the great flood of 2012, as had been most of the world. History did travel and some knowledge was never lost to time. Something Mateo was grateful for. It had been said that samurais would battle each other with the style and that fascinated Mateo.

Over the three weeks that he'd been able to interact with the gladiators, he'd learned their names and where they'd come from, how long they'd been there. Some had been there since they were children, growing up at the ludus, like Gregor. Boris had been taken from the lushlands of Soria in the celestial city of Gemini.

During their discussions, the men had already given up hope of ever being freed and the only freedom they sought now was a glorious death in the arena, which did come to one of the gladiators at the last Games. Mateo didn't know Sonder well, but he was still saddened by his death. Sonder's lover, however, had moved on to another gladiator's bed. Mateo didn't bother to think much on it, since maybe it was Liam's way of coping with a loss that could come at any time, even to himself.

Mateo had learned a lot in three weeks, like why they only had candles and not electric lamps. Their dominus was wealthy enough to own a ludus, but not wealthy enough to move up in status like other men and women the gods had given favor to. The ones who upheld the laws and kept the humans in line. Those in power. They could afford such luxuries. It was explained to Mateo that Rama hoped to one day be amongst the elite through the glory of his house.

With each victory, Rama came one step closer to his goal, which was why his gladiators had to be the best in the land. Knowing this information now, he understood why Rama had given him to Eloy for pleasure. He wondered just how much favor his virgin ass brought their detestable dominus. The thought made him hate Rama even more.

After the long day of training, they ate dinner, then it was bath time. Mateo learned that these little pleasures were something to be indulged in. Moments that belonged to them. Lunch, dinner, and bath time. These were moments when they weren't constantly watched. Where orders weren't given, unless out of necessity. Where they could be free while still in captivity. He'd learned to enjoy these moments too.

He sat in the tub, washing the sweat, blood, and dirt from his arm, and examined the thin cut over his bicep, which was now more muscular than it had been a month ago. He wasn't a waif to begin with, it had been said to him that he came from good stock. His body was already muscular naturally because of all the hard work it took to live in the badlands. But he was starting to see progress in his physique that he did like.

Out of nowhere, Titus, the current champion of the ludus, climbed into the tub next to him, smiling. "It doesn't look bad," he said, gesturing to the wound.

Mateo looked at the cut on his arm again and nodded. "Yes. It was stupid of me. A mistake I'll not repeat."

"Smart," Titus said. "Let me get your back."

Mateo started to get an uneasy feeling, knowing where this interaction could be heading. Still, he turned, allowing the champion gladiator to wash his back. When the man's hand reach lower to his ass cheeks, he turned back around.

"Gratitude, Titus," he said, not wanting to insult the champion of the house. His last fight had sent a surge of amazement through the crowd, it was said. He'd killed his opponent in record time, much to the dismay of the house of Elise, whose female gladiators were extremely formidable. So, Titus' miraculous win would surely go down in history as one of the greatest matches. For his reward, he was given to the goddess, Odessa, for her pleasure.

The smile on Titus' face widened as he moved closer, pressing his chest to Mateo's arm. He leaned over near his ear. "Let us give each other ecstasy," he said. "I've been watching you, you have skill. Let me mentor you."

Mateo was more naive of the way things worked when he had first gotten to the ludus, but he was much wiser now and the meaning behind Titus' words didn't escape him. He'd once heard the term mentioned before when listening to two gladiators making a trade. "Quid pro quo". Basically, nothing was free, and if you do for me, I'll do for you. If he had sex with Titus, the gladiator would help him train.

Would that be something he could turn down? Only a fool would. He wanted to survive. Wanted to live past his test to meet his first opponent on the sands. He wanted to be the best of the best so that one day, he could gain his freedom the way Rama had.

He turned to Titus. "Here?" he asked, making a decision he hoped he wouldn't regret.

Titus shrugged as if to say, why not? "Sure. You're not shy, are you?"

He'd long since gotten over whatever shyness he had. Looking around, some men were watching them, while others were tending to their own needs and desires. Mateo looked back at Titus. "Let us do it in the corner, over there, with the oil."

Titus turned and looked at the empty corner and nodded. He climbed out first, then helped Mateo. They walked over to the corner, grabbing a bottle of passion oil along the way. They had several different kinds of oil they could use, but this one was the favorite among the men who often fucked in the baths. It was said to heat up with friction, making sex more intense.

Mateo wasn't sure intense sex was something he wanted to experience, but he would use it anyway, especially if it got him what he wanted. Training from a champion. He poured some oil onto his fingers, then slipped them inside of his asshole, while Titus oiled up his cock.

Mateo looked over his shoulder, watching Titus, but over *his* shoulder, he could see Boris looking on. The gladiator's gaze was full of rage and jealousy, but he dared not approach. Titus being champion of the ludus gave him privileges the others didn't have. For instance, he had his own room next to Cervantes. The food he ate was of better quality than theirs. He was allowed to have more possessions, and when he spoke, other gladiators listened and followed orders.

Kodac was his friend and second only to him in the ludus as far as skill went, which was why he'd gained Rama's favor and why he held a higher position over the gladiators, too. He was Cervantes' assistant and had also trained Mateo, as well as the others. Mateo hoped that by fucking Titus, it would keep him from having to ward off the others, which he'd been doing with great difficulty. The men were quite hungry for his body and didn't seem to like being rejected.

"Relax," Titus said as he aimed the head of his cock against Mateo's asshole.

Before turning back around, Mateo had gotten a good look at the cock that was about to breach him. Nine inches and thick, though cut. Titus wasn't one of the men who repulsed him, so he hoped he wouldn't become one after they had sex. This was the first time he was going to have sex with others watching, and that alone made him a little nervous.

"Relax," Titus repeated. "It'll hurt more if you are this stiff."

"I'm sorry. Never did it in front of people before," Mateo said.

"Now's a good time to start," Titus said.

Mateo blew out the air in his lungs as Titus pressed forward, the tip of his cock breaking past his sphincter. Mateo grunted as he was stretched again. Since losing his virginity, he'd had sex with three males. Eloy, his first. Cervantes and Rama. The last being five times, and thanks to the lesson Cervantes had taught him in the hallway that night, he was able to get hard when Rama was fucking him.

Unfortunately, that never resulted in an orgasm for him, and Rama seemed to care less if it did. Only that his cock inside of him made Mateo aroused. Mateo realized that Rama's ego needed to be stroked just as vigilantly as his cock did.

He continued to breathe slowly as Titus pushed his cock deeper inside of him until the gladiator's hips pressed against his ass cheeks, and both men shuddered. There was a curve to Titus's cock that brushed along something inside Mateo's ass that felt good. Something he'd felt from time to time when he'd been fucked before, but nothing ever came of it. He wondered what that thing was.

"Just relax," Titus said again as he began pumping his cock inside Mateo's hole. "Ooohh, so tight."

Those words were something Mateo had been used to hearing. Rama said them every time they fucked.

"I know," Mateo said, then moaned as Titus' cock grazed that spot again and again, making him feel something amazing for the first time. He pressed both hands against the wall, keeping his ass pushed out for Titus to fuck, but his cock began to grow hard all on its own without thoughts of Eloy to help. The phenomenon astonished Mateo, as he had never had it happen this way before.

Titus laughed through his heavy pants. "You like my cock?" It was more of a statement than a question, but Mateo answered.

"Yes," he said, and it was the first time he didn't have to lie when those words were spoken to him. He actually felt pleasure in his ass where Titus' cock stroked inside of him.

"I want to see you cum," Titus purred, then reached around Mateo, grabbing his cock.

This was another new experience, the dual pleasure, one inside and out. His nails scraped along the clay wall as he continued to brace himself as Titus fucked him. He could hear some of the other gladiators cheering Titus on as he fucked him. Knowing they were being watched gave Mateo an array of feelings. Embarrassment and arousal on the same level. He was nervous and excited to know others were watching him experience something so intimate and for the first time, pleasurable. He could hear his own moans and grunts mixing with Titus', and he could also feel his body reaching the point of no return.

Titus growled as his hand furiously stroked Mateo's cock. "Yeah, you're ready. Shoot it all over the wall."

That was going to be inevitable, as he was facing the wall as his balls drew up. Titus laughed as Mateo moaned louder and then quaked as he reached his orgasm. His cock squirted thick, white ropes of cum all over the wall, and he looked down to see his seed running down the wall in rivulets.

"Oh… Ooohh, so hot… makes my balls boil," Titus declared, then he released Mateo's cock to grip his hair, yanking Mateo's head back.

"Fuck his cunt good, Titus!" several gladiators roared.

One even walked over to them and patted Titus on the back as he continued to pound Mateo's asshole. Mateo managed to look out the corner of his eye to see their new voyeur was Helix, a friend of Titus' too. The blond, blue-eyed gladiator grinned as he watched Titus' cock, glistening with oil, plunge in and out of Mateo's firm, plump mounds.

"Mmmm, I'm next," he said.

Titus laughed as if giving his permission to something that wasn't his to give. Mateo only agreed to let Titus fuck him, he didn't see anything to gain from letting his friend, not that he had a problem with Helix.

"About to fill him up," Titus announced, then his thrusts became more erratic right before his body stiffened and he roared like a beast.

Mateo could feel Titus' cock swell inside of him, stretching his anal walls a bit more right before the flood came. Titus' cumload was quite impressive, something he expected from a gladiator with balls as large as he had. He could feel Titus' cum running down his inner thighs as the gladiator continued to milk his cock inside of him. Titus shuddered one last time, then pulled out, leaving Mateo exposed. Helix stepped in Titus' place as the other gladiator backed away, but that was when Mateo turned around, facing them.

"I fuck Titus, not you," he told Helix, who frowned.

Titus stepped up, brushing his fingers along Mateo's cheek. "With a cunt as sweet as yours, my friend should taste it."

Cervantes was right, the boy was gone and in his place was the man Mateo was forced to become. Weakness would be exploited, this he was learning. Conviction would be an asset to him.

He shook his head. "Not yours to share."

"Who do you think you are?" Helix snarled. "You don't even bare the mark of a man… a gladiator." He held up his arm to show the brand of Rama's crest on his inner forearm. "You have no rank."

"I'm not a gladiator…yet. But I'm not your slave, either," Mateo said. He pushed Helix back, sending the gladiator stumbling into Titus.

Helix growled as his face contorted in anger. He lunged for Mateo, but Titus held him back. "Let me go!"

"Fuck another's cunt, Helix." Titus grabbed Helix's cock and balls as he turned him around to face the other gladiators. "Who wants some of this?" he asked the crowd as he gave the man's genitals a few shakes.

A few of the men laughed, some waved him over, and that was when Titus released Helix and pushed him off in the direction of the gladiators willing to give Helix a go. He then turned back to Mateo, who was still standing his ground. He walked up to him, backing him against the wall, and placed both hands on either side of Mateo.

"You surprise," he said.

"I'm not yours to share with your friends," Mateo warned.

Titus smiled and nodded. "One day, maybe you change your mind?"

Mateo looked at him. "About fucking your friends?"

Titus shook his head. "About being mine."

Not likely, Mateo thought. He was already a slave, he wasn't going to give up what little rights he did have to become the bedmate slave of a gladiator.

"Not your slave," he reiterated.

"Not slave, but lover," Titus corrected.

Mateo didn't see how anyone could have a relationship under such circumstances as they were in. But he also didn't have those feelings for Titus. He wanted to learn from the man, not become his lover.

"Tomorrow, you will train me?" Mateo asked, getting back to what was important to him, why he'd given in to the gladiator in the first place.

"You keep this up, you survive. Tomorrow, yes." Titus realized what Mateo wanted and he had to give the nineteen-year-old credit. He was a far cry from the terrified boy he had been when he'd first laid eyes on him. On the contrary, Mateo was learning the game of life in the celestial cities. He laughed and slapped Mateo's ass, then gripped the cheek, giving it a little jiggle. "Tomorrow night, we fuck." If this was their deal, he was going to milk it.

Mateo nodded, and Titus released him, letting Mateo finish bathing. The other gladiators carried on doing whatever they were doing until it was time for bed. Mateo climbed onto his cot and closed his eyes. He was looking forward to getting training from not only Cervantes, but also from Titus the next morning. The more he knew, the better his chances would be.

CHAPTER ELEVEN

"**Y**ou drop your shoulder every time you go to thrust," Titus chastised.

"Which shoulder?" Mateo asked, looking from one shoulder to the other.

"Your right when you thrust. You fight with both swords, your opponent shouldn't know how you're going to attack," Titus said. "Block with one sword, keep your shoulders straight, thrust with the other."

Mateo took the lesson to heart, making a conscious effort not to give his moves away. He and Titus sparred for hours before lunch time. Both men had worked up quite a sweat, and in Titus' case, quite the sexual appetite. Mateo waited in line for his bowl of oatmeal and when he got up to the pot, a spoonful of human shit was given to him.

"Gladiators eat stew. Slaves eat what came out of my ass," the cook said.

Mateo looked at him, frowning in disgust. "We're all slaves."

"Some more valuable than others," the man shot back.

"He'll eat what I eat," Titus said, then steeled his stance, challenging the man to refuse.

"You got your cock wet in his cunt and now he's special?" the cook said.

"Cornelius, do you desire my foot in your ass?" Titus warned.

The man snarled a snaggle-tooth frown. "I reckon not. Fine." Grudgingly, he took the bowl from Mateo's hands that had the feces in it and gave him a new bowl with fresh stew. The aroma of the food drifted up to his nostrils and made his stomach growl in anticipation.

"Wise. And the next time you do that, I'll make you eat it," Titus warned, then took his bowl of chicken soup, which had been made with half a chicken, and two pieces of bread, then walked Mateo over to his table where Kodac and Helix were sitting.

"Sit," Titus said, gesturing to the seat next to his.

Mateo took his seat and Titus gave him one of the pieces of bread. "Gratitude." Already, he was benefiting from having sex with the champion of the house. God knew he didn't want to eat the stale oatmeal he had been eating while being forced to watch the gladiators enjoy stews, soups, and even mixed vegetables. And he sure as fuck wasn't going to eat Cornelius' shit.

"Do you think he…" Mateo wondered if the cook put his feces anywhere else. The thought made him want to vomit, so he decided not to ask.

Titus chuckled. "Not if he wants his life," he said, guessing what Mateo was going to ask. "Eat up, it's good and safe."

Mateo dipped his bread into the stew with the potatoes, carrots, peas, and beef cubes, then took a bite. He didn't moan in pleasure at the taste, but he wanted to. It wasn't as good as anything his mom could have made with a fresh kill from a successful hunt, but it was better than what he'd been eating for weeks.

"I wouldn't get too attached," Helix said.

Mateo looked up at the brooding gladiator who was glaring at him, obviously still cross that he'd been rejected the night before. "To what?" he asked.

"For you, to all this," Helix gestured to the bowl of stew Mateo was eating. Then he turned his gaze to Titus. "To you—him, as I doubt he'll survive the test."

"Even with me training him?" Titus asked with a smirk. He didn't let his friend's grumpy attitude affect him.

Helix snorted and looked back at Mateo. "When your cunt is used up, he'll be done with you."

Mateo swallowed the food he had in his mouth, then replied, "And even then, I still wouldn't want your cock inside me."

Titus and Kodac laughed at the young man's comeback.

"He might just have more of a chance than we expect," Kodac said, grinning as he ate his meal.

Mateo smiled as he took another spoonful of his stew. He was more determined than they were giving him credit for, but he also didn't mind that he'd been underestimated. As Cervantes had told him, "Let your enemy think less of you, so that when you do attack, they are caught off guard". That was what he was going to do.

After lunch, they continued their training. Titus was put on strength training, and he sparred with Cervantes who noted the differences in his progress. But with seeing the improvement, also came tougher lessons, and Mateo found himself face-first in the sand several times. His nose busted and head throbbing from blows he did not see coming. All mistakes he planned on not repeating. The hours were long and grueling, and at the end of the day, he was sore and tired.

The gladiators were dismissed and the men shuffled off to the baths to relax and bathe, among other things. Mateo soaked in the tub, allowing the warm water to pamper his aching body. His eyes were closed as his head rested against the edge, but he opened them the moment he felt someone approaching.

Titus was grinning down at him as he waded through the water towards his target. He pressed his body against Mateo's and leaned down, kissing him. Mateo returned his kiss, letting his tongue slip into Titus' mouth to caress his. Titus growled, his lust evident and demanding as he pushed himself between Mateo's legs.

"I've wanted to be inside you all day," he said, still grinning.

"I've seen your gaze upon me. I know its intent, but I only want to bathe," Mateo said.

Titus frowned, his brown eyebrows creasing. "Perhaps tomorrow, you will eat oatmeal. Perhaps I'll train another."

Mateo didn't need to have it spelled out for him what Titus meant. "Are you not tired?"

"No, I am horny." He reached into the water, grabbing Mateo's legs, and hoisted them around his waist. "My cock hardens with one look at you."

Mateo could feel Titus' erection poking at his asshole and he knew if he wanted to continue to get perks, he was going to have to continue down this path he'd chosen. He braced himself on the edge of the tub just as Titus pushed his cock inside of him. The gladiator pounded him harder than he had the night before, almost as if he was somehow claiming Mateo in some animalistic mating ritual.

The pleasure Mateo had felt before was missing this time, and he had to go back to that place where he often traveled to think of something that would make him aroused. He didn't think Titus would like the fact that his cock remained flaccid as he fucked him. Again, Mateo's thoughts drifted back to Eloy, the god who was far more beautiful and impressive than any man. Although he could be just as cruel, that wasn't what Mateo focused on. Always, it went back to fantasy. To the gentle touches, the smile Eloy had given him. The eyes that looked at him as if he was special. That was what he held on to as Titus rammed his cock in and out of his asshole.

"Ahh, fuuck!" Titus growled as he quaked against Mateo. The water splashed between the two men as one reached his explosive climax. Titus roared and cursed again as he came, relishing every second of it. He'd fucked every man in there, but Mateo's body yielded the most pleasure. He was going to claim Mateo whether the man agreed or not, for as long as they both lived under the same roof.

Huffing and puffing, he pulled his softening cock out of Mateo's asshole, satisfied he'd gotten pleasure. "Now, you can bathe," he said, as if giving Mateo permission.

Mateo didn't bother to comment, thinking it was best to let Titus feel that he was in control. He would use the gladiator's benefits as the gladiator used his body for pleasure. The other gladiators didn't bother to try to approach them, and that was just another perk to Mateo. If they thought he belonged to Titus, then perhaps they would cease their constant advances. That was something Mateo could appreciate.

He finished bathing and cleaned out his asshole as best he could. When it was time to rest, Titus had demanded he sleep in the cot next to his, so he did. Again, the other men didn't say anything, and Mateo knew this was a new beginning for him.

Three months passed with Titus training and fucking Mateo and Mateo gaining the knowledge and privilege he desired. It wasn't entirely bad to give himself to Titus physically. For the most part, he could orgasm, even if he did have to fantasize about Eloy to achieve it. It all was worthwhile as far as Mateo was concerned. His body was taller and even more toned than when he'd first arrived at the ludus.

His muscles were thicker and more defined. His body had bulked up to the point where he was no longer considered the 'little bird' by Boris, who was the gladiator he would have to face for his test. Now, the gladiator called him 'little man', even though he stood six feet. Progress was progress. Of course, Boris still wanted to fuck Mateo, but wouldn't dare cross Titus, who was even more popular after having won every match he'd been in, keeping his champion status intact.

"Are you nervous?" Titus asked him as he wrapped up Mateo's hands and wrists with strips of leather.

Mateo nodded. "I am. I have to defeat Boris or die."

Titus nodded. "I would be very disappointed if you died."

Mateo looked up at him and smirked. "You'd only miss a warm place for your cock."

Titus laughed and shrugged. "I would miss that, yes. But I think we mean more than that to each other."

Mateo knew better, though. Had he refused to fuck Titus, the gladiator would have ceased paying him attention. Sure, as long as he continued to be his lover, Titus could claim their relationship was built on something other than sex, but that was only if Mateo stayed in his place. Mateo had tested those waters before, and every time he did not want to have sex, Titus had punished him. Either he wouldn't train him the next day, or he would allow the cook to give Mateo the less desirable meal.

Mateo had been in the ludus four months and he was no fool. He'd learned a lot of the ways of men, and he refused to let them break him. Still, if Titus wanted to believe he could mean anything more to Mateo than an easier life and better training, then so be it.

Mateo smiled and leaned forward, kissing Titus. "We do," he lied.

Titus smirked as he tied off the leather. "Boris has a weakness in his defense to the left."

Mateo nodded, taking the hint. "Gratitude."

Titus smiled, then looked down at Mateo, their gazes locked. "Do you know why I fight so hard?"

"For the glory of this house and to give worship to the gods?" Mateo supplied.

Titus shrugged. "Goes with the territory. I fight because I want to go down in history as one of the greatest gladiators to have lived. I want my monument to stand outside the arena along with the other greats, and for people to gaze upon it and aspire to be as great as I was. History is created by those brave enough to tell its story."

The words Titus had spoken were so profound to Mateo, and he did find them inspiring. Although, he wanted to go down in history as one of the gladiators so amazing that he earned his own freedom. That was the story he wanted to tell.

He smiled at Titus again. "Gratitude."

"It's time," Cervantes announced.

Mateo took a deep breath, then followed Titus to the courtyard where all of the gladiators had gathered and formed a circle. Mateo walked to the center of the circle and stood before Cervantes.

"Now, we see if you took to my lessons," Cervantes said, then gestured for Boris to join them.

The hulking beast of a gladiator walked into the middle of the circle and smiled at Mateo. "I take it easy on you if you promise to fuck me."

"Shameful, Boris," Cervantes said.

"I'll spare his life, then, better?" Boris asked, looking at Cervantes, who shook his head.

"I'll spare your life if you stop asking," Mateo said.

Cervantes laughed and gestured for both men to face the ludus where their dominus was standing on the balcony, watching them. "Pay your respects to your dominus."

All of the gladiators faced Rama and chanted his name in a thunderous chorus. Mateo had joined them, though he did not respect the man who'd continued to keep him oppressed. Rama smiled as he listened to his slaves give him the glorious praise. He raised his hand, silencing them.

"Tonight, we will see if you were worth the rubios I paid for you, slave. If you survive tonight's test, but fail, I will sell you to the first brothel who would have you," Rama told Mateo.

Mateo bowed his head. "I will not fail, dominus." If he wasn't already motivated to win, the threat of being sold into a brothel added extra incentive.

"Let us see," Rama said, then nodded for Cervantes to continue.

"Weapons," Cervantes announced, and two slaves ran over to both men, handing them their swords.

Boris took hold of the hilt to his massive broadsword. Mateo was used to seeing the brute wield it and he understood what Titus said when he mentioned Boris' weakness, one that he was surely going to exploit. Looking at them, one would think that their match was a bit one-sided, as Boris' big sword looked far deadlier than Mateo's twin blades, but each gladiator had been trained to be able to stand their ground with their individual weapons. It was not supposed to matter if one opponent had a sword and a blade while the other had only a rapier or sai. It didn't matter if one was taller or more muscular than the other. Or male verses a female gladiator. Each were considered evenly matched if they had been trained properly.

Mateo gripped the handles of his two swords and faced Boris. His heart was racing a mile a minute, as he knew this was a moment of truth. If he didn't succeed, he'd rather die by Boris' blade than live to see his body be sold. Every lesson he'd been taught filled his thoughts because he didn't want to make one mistake that could seal his fate for the worse.

Boris was watching Mateo with a mixture of lust and revenge, perhaps he'd use his blade to punish Mateo for all the times he'd rejected him. If the boy did manage to survive, he was planning on taking what he wanted from Mateo. If he was to be sold to a brothel, it would make him an even lesser slave than he was and even Titus couldn't protect him. The thought made Boris smile.

Cervantes stepped away as two slaves poured oil in a circle around the two men. Another gladiator handed Cervantes a lit torch. "The rules are simple. Two men enter, and the one who falls through the fire loses. If one kills the other, you also win." He lit the oil, igniting a ring of fire around Mateo and Boris. "Let the test begin!"

All of the other gladiators stepped back a little as the flames grew and crackled. Mateo and Boris sized each other up as they circled one another, waiting for the moment to attack. Mateo's palms were sweaty, but the leather binding them helped him keep his grip steady on his blades. Their eyes settled on one another and Mateo winked, which sent Boris into a rage.

The monstrous gladiator charged at him, swinging his sword that was almost as tall as he was. It took every bit of Boris' massive muscles to wield the thing and Mateo, being smaller and lighter on his feet, dodged the first swing with ease. Boris followed up his attack with an overhead swing, which Mateo blocked by bringing both of his blades together to form an X. Pushing up, he forced Boris to step back.

"You gonna get this cock," Boris threatened as he grabbed his crotch with his free hand, wiggling it at Mateo.

Mateo didn't bother to feed into the taunt, refusing to become distracted by trivial things. This was his second match to the death he'd had, and this time, Eloy wouldn't be there to save him. He had to rely on his own wits and skills.

Again, the two clashed swords, and Mateo had to struggle harder when Boris pressed on his blade, attempting to slice Mateo in two. Both men grunted, their chests heaving as they battled. Already, the match had gone on longer than most had expected.

Mateo kicked Boris in his face, knocking the gladiator back long enough for him to take his offensive stance back. His shoulder bled a little where Boris' blade had made contact. It was time for Mateo to switch up his style from defensive to offensive and throw Boris off his game. Where Boris had raw strength and body mass, Mateo had speed and agility.

Mateo focused on Boris' weakness and attacked at his left side, blocking the gladiator's blade with his, while using his short sword to slice Boris on his side. Several gladiators cheered Mateo on, happy to see that he'd made such a blow, Titus being among them. Again, Boris swung his blade and Mateo ducked, lest he lose his head. Seeing that Boris had left his chest open, Mateo turned into him, slicing his blade across Boris' pec, leaving a deep gash.

"Arg!" Boris groaned as he stumbled back, gripping his now bleeding wound. He glared at Mateo with even more rage, and Mateo hoped to use that anger to his advantage.

"I see now why you did not go to the last two Games," Mateo teased, tossing a few insults of his own to get Boris even more enraged.

"You cunt!" Boris yelled, then charged at Mateo.

Keeping on his toes, Mateo bounced back as Boris rushed at him. He made sure to steer clear of the flames that licked at them, as he didn't want to lose by falling out of the ring. He dodged and sliced Boris across his back, and the gladiator cried out, but countered with an elbow to Mateo's temple, knocking him dizzy. Mateo fell back, his body hitting the sands with a hard thud. Boris was on him, seeking to take advantage of the blow he'd given. Mateo rolled out of the way of Boris' blade as it sliced through the air.

Quickly, Mateo climbed to his feet, shaking the cobwebs of disorientation free. His head was throbbing and it was a bit harder for him to concentrate, but he forced himself to stay focused. Again, Boris came at him, sword swinging. Mateo leaped low, slicing Boris' left leg to the bone.

"Ahhhh, fuck!" Boris yelled as he collapsed to one knee, his other leg bleeding out as a puddle of blood formed beneath him.

Mateo couldn't believe his good fortune at having brought down the giant on such a risky maneuver. That one weakness Boris had on his left was paying off. He climbed to his feet, attacking Boris hard. The huge gladiator blocked several of Mateo's offensive thrusts, but couldn't defend against them all, and had been sliced and cut several times by one sword or the other as Mateo worked his dual sword techniques.

Boris swung his huge sword wildly and Mateo dodged his attacks by jumping back or to the left. When he saw his opening, he lunged forward, his blade making its mark through Boris' throat. The crowd hushed as blood bubbled up from Boris' mouth. Mateo's mouth dropped open as his eyes bulged, shocked by his first victory, and one against a seasoned gladiator. He pulled his blade free and more blood gushed from the wound and began flowing down Boris' hairy chest.

The gladiator gurgled one last time before his body fell face first into the sand, his huge broadsword falling last. Mateo stood over Boris' body, the heat from the flames making him sweat even more as he panted from the exhaustion that was now taking over his limbs. He hadn't even realized how much energy he'd spent fighting, as he was running on pure adrenaline during the battle.

Everything seemed so surreal as he stared at the blood oozing from Boris' corpse. He'd won, he'd actually defeated one of their better gladiators. He wouldn't go so far as to call Boris the best, Haraka was better, but still… this was a fight people did not think he'd win, and he had. There was hope.

Three slaves ran toward the ring of fire as some of the gladiators broke out in applause and cheers. The slaves began kicking sand over the lit oil, extinguishing the flames enough so Mateo could step out of the smoldering ring. Cervantes walked up to him and nodded once, then looked at Boris' corpse. He took Mateo's hand, raising it in victory.

"Your winner!" he yelled, and the gladiators applauded louder. Titus cheered as he clapped. Cervantes turned to Mateo. "I'll be honest, I wasn't sure you'd win. You are now a gladiator, and you will be branded as one."

The branding ceremony wasn't something Mateo had been looking forward to, but it was something he wanted only because it meant he'd survived his test and could move forward towards the road to reclaiming his freedom.

"Gratitude for your training, doctore," Mateo said, giving the man his due credit.

"Good you listened," Cervantes replied, then he turned to see the slaves removing Boris' corpse off the sand. They carried the body inside the ludus. His broadsword was left on the sand, still with Mateo's blood on the blade from when Boris had gotten in a few good licks. "It was an impressive victory and Boris died honorably."

"He did, doctore," Mateo agreed. But in the back of his mind, he was happy that it was Boris' corpse being carried away instead of his, or worse yet, his injured body being carted off to a seedy brothel.

"Honor thy fallen brother!" Cervantes yelled, and the other gladiators shouted Boris' name three times and the gladiator mantra of "fortune favored the gods and was favored by the gods". Mateo had joined them in the chant.

"Mateo has proven himself tonight as one of you. He will now take the brand of our dominus," Cervantes announced to the roar of the gladiators. He turned to Mateo. "Kneel and present arm."

Mateo did as he was commanded, dropping to both knees and holding his right arm up, forearm exposed. He knew where the brand was going to go and knew it would hurt. Cervantes walked over to an iron bowl that was lit with fire and had the branding iron roasting inside. Using thick leather gloves, he reached for the iron, removing it from the fire. The insignia for the House of Rama was at the tip of the iron. An intricate shield with two swords crossing over the "R".

Mateo took several deep breaths as he prepared himself for the searing pain he knew was coming. He also knew he'd have to recite the oath that went with the brand. A pledge of loyalty to a life he didn't want nor had he asked for, but it was his destiny, as his fate would have it. So, to that, he would make the most of it. That was the real pledge he would make to himself tonight as he said the other words.

Cervantes held the smoking, red hot iron in one hand as he gripped Mateo's wrist with the other. "Speak these words of oath after me with your answer."

Mateo nodded. "Yes, doctore."

"Do you promise to serve the House of Rama in glorious battle in the arena until the day of your death?"

He didn't like the words, they implied he would never see freedom and it made him wonder how seven gladiators had broken the chains of slavery before him. Still, he had no choice in the matter and he repeated the words that felt hollow to him.

"I do promise to give my life to the House of Rama in glorious battle," Mateo said.

"Do you promise to make each battle in the arena a victory, even unto death, to the House of Rama to elevate it?" Cervantes asked.

Mateo nodded. "Yes, doctore. I promise to make every victory, even in death, a glory to the House of Rama."

"Do you promise to serve your dominus in any way he sees fit?"

Mateo forced himself not to groan as he hated having to serve Rama, period. But the dominus had already taken quite advantage of the fact that Mateo was a slave and he—his master.

"Yes, I promise to serve my dominus," Mateo said.

"Do you promise to honor your brothers in this ludus and in the arena?"

Mateo nodded. "Yes, I promise to honor my gladiator brothers in the ludus and in the arena."

"Do you promise to give all glory to the gods, as well as the House of Rama, keeping none for yourself?" Cervantes asked the final question Mateo must pledge to.

Glory to the gods? He'd met a god and saw very little reason to give him his glory. Although, perhaps he had to give Eloy his gratitude as he was the reason why Mateo was alive today.

Mateo nodded. "I will give all glory to the four celestial gods and to the House of Rama, keeping none for myself."

With that, Cervantes was satisfied, as was Rama, who nodded, giving Cervantes permission to brand Mateo. He pressed the smoking brand to Mateo's flesh, sizzling it as Mateo gritted his teeth together to keep from screaming in pain like he wanted to do. Finally, the iron was removed and the brand was now in place. Mateo looked at his burned skin and at the design forever emblazoned on it. He tried not to think of it as permanent, because he still had hope that one day... he would be free.

Part two continues in Destiny: Gods and Slaves.
WWW.NICHOLASBELLA.COM

CPSIA information can be obtained
at www.ICGtesting.com
Printed in the USA
LVHW090211240222
711893LV00012B/129